NO SECOND CHANCES

KATE EVANGELISTA

READS

SWOON READS | NEW YORK

A SWOON READS BOOK

An imprint of Feiwel and Friends and Macmillan Publishing Group, LLC

Our books may be purchased in bulk for promotional, educational, or
business use. Please contact your local bookseller or the Macmillan Corporate
and Premium Sales Department at (800) 221-7945 ext. 5442 or by e-mail at
MacmillanSpecialMarkets@macmillan.com.

Library of Congress Cataloging-in-Publication Data is available.

ISBN 978-1-250-10067-2 (paperback) / ISBN 978-1-250-10068-9 (ebook)

Book design by Liz Dresner

First edition—2017

10 9 8 7 6 5 4 3 2

swoonreads.com

For soul mates . . .
Because even vast distances cannot separate them.

True love allowed each person to follow their own path,
knowing that they would never lose touch with their Soul Mate.

—PAULO COELHO, *BRIDA*

Prologue

JACKSON MALLORY LIVED to hold people's hearts in his hands. Not literally, of course. Once he discovered it was possible through music, he never looked back. The magic number was 128 BPM: the beats per minute most in sync with a person's heart rate when dancing. Matching that primal pulse was always his primary goal when headlining a dance party.

At a former church turned nightclub called Paradiso in the heart of Amsterdam, Jackson was at the top of his game. A worldwide tour. Several tracks climbing the charts. Artists wanting to collaborate. Asking for anything more seemed like tempting fate to take it all away.

Jackson in the DJ booth wasn't a performance. It was a show. The smoke machines and strobe lights were all timed to his beats. He liked to start slow, with a bass line people moved their hips to. Then he built on that, like a house—brick by brick. In his case, it was layers of sound until he reached 120 BPM. Approximately the heartbeat of a long-distance runner. Once there, he gradually raised the bar song by song, coaxing the crowd to move with him. Obey his every whim and command.

Every so often he picked up the mic and addressed the crush. Their hoots and shouts of adoration fueled him. It was the life. His life. What he had been working toward since he first started recording all the sounds around him, catching each note like a boy with a butterfly net.

During a gig, he liked focusing on one person. Man or woman, it didn't matter. What he looked for was a sense of rhythm. Something he curated his music around. In his mind, if he changed the way that person moved, his job was done for the night.

On that cool September night, his eyes landed on the most beautiful sight—sunrises on the beach of Ibiza couldn't compare. In the space packed to the brim with liquored-up, drugged-up, gyrating bodies, she stood out. The embodiment of the wonder he'd felt the first time he heard the cuckoo clock his mother brought home from Germany when he was five years old. That clock changed everything. It brought music into his world. And like the music, she brought magic into his life.

Natasha Parker. Dodge Cove princess. In the tightest leather dress and the highest heels Jackson had ever seen. She moved that sexy body to the beat. *His* beat. Her sable hair bounced with each jump. Hands in the air, she swayed. Her bee-stung lips in a perfect pout.

If he were to describe dancing as bands, some people danced like the Rolling Stones, rock stars who shoot from the hip.

Others danced like Daft Punk, all disco-fueled foot movements and jerky arms. Natasha . . . Well, she was Marvin Gaye all the way. All smooth sensuality—moves that flowed with the music as if her body was the lyrics.

The acrid smoke, the bright lasers, the hypersonic beats faded away. His focus went to the melody she created with every grind of her hips. With the pumping of her chest. With the weaving of her fingers above her head as if she plucked the notes he created for herself.

Not taking his eyes off her, Jackson transitioned into a pre-recorded song. He hated doing it, since he liked curating the set while spinning—mixing songs depending on the vibe of the room. But he had to get close to her. Had to prove to himself she was real.

Setting aside his headphones, he jumped down from the booth and snaked his way to her through the whirling mass. The club was dark enough that no one really recognized him. Plus, they were already deep into the night. The molly and whatever else they were taking had long past kicked in.

Like the night he first discovered what being a DJ meant at his brother's party many years ago, Jackson stood and watched. The way Natasha moved should have been considered illegal. The thoughts she inspired in him were certainly bad, naughty, dirty things. He had seen his fair share of women in various stages of undress dancing to his music, but none of them compared to the goddess a yard from him.

He wanted to fall on his knees and worship her.

She had her eyes closed and her lips pursed. It seemed like she was really feeling the music with a graceful sex appeal that called to Jackson. Without having to think twice, he moved toward her. She turned around, her backside facing him. He placed his hands on her hips and pulled her against his chest.

Natasha gasped. She whirled to face him. Her crystal-blue eyes, lined thickly with black eyeliner, grew wide. A lock of hair clung to the light sweat on her forehead. He reached out to smooth the strands away, but she recoiled like a cat about to strike.

"Are you real?" Jackson asked, in awe. "Because if this is a dream, I don't ever want to wake up."

"Oh, I'm real, all right," she said, stance wide, arms crossed.

"It's so good to see you."

"I wish I could say the same."

He gave her a once-over. Her cheeks were flushed. She was breathing hard. And her eyes . . . there was no describing the heated emotion in them.

Making a snap decision, he grabbed her hand and tugged her off the dance floor, ignoring her protests. The main room was too loud. It was one of the only times when music wasn't his friend.

On the way to the exit, his phone vibrated in his pocket. He fished it out and glanced at the screen. It was a text from Preston.

> Natasha is at the club tonight. Can you make sure she gets home safely?

He pulled Natasha through the first set of doors that led outside, texting with his free hand.

> I'll do that.

They faced each other in the space between two doors, barely bigger than a coat closet. Behind Natasha, the booming bass still pushed through. The harsh fluorescent lighting above them let out a faint buzz, flickering every once in a while.

"What do you think you're doing?" Natasha asked.

Jackson slid the phone into his back pocket, then ran his fingers through his damp hair. "You won't believe how happy I am right now. When I saw you in the crowd tonight—"

She jerked back. "Happy?"

"Yeah. I missed you. So much."

"Miss me? You *miss* me?"

"Yeah." He reached out for her, but she moved away. "My heart is beating so hard right now I think I'm going to pass out. You should feel it."

"You're a sick bastard, do you know that?" She crossed her arms again, her brow furrowed.

Jackson's brow mimicked Natasha's. "I don't understand."

A laugh escaped her lips as she shook her head. "Well, let me make things clear for you. You left. No word."

"If you let me explain—"

"What's there to explain? It looks pretty obvious to me." She pointed toward the club. "That's your life now."

"Can you hear yourself right now?"

"You seriously think I'm being crazy?" She slapped her forehead with the heel of her hand and laughed until she doubled over.

All the blood rushed to the pads of Jackson's feet as he slowly realized what was happening. "Come on, Tash. Let's talk about this."

"Talk?" Natasha sobered. "Now, after all this time, you

want to talk?" She cut her hand through the air between them. "No. I only came to prove to myself that I'm over you."

"Tash, don't do this. Please."

She sized him up with those eyes he'd once thought could tame any man's wild heart. They absolutely conquered his.

"No second chances," she said, finality in her tone.

The words were a slap in the face. They stunned him into silence.

With all the dignity in the world, she lifted her chin before she turned around and stalked off, leaving the scent of her expensive perfume behind.

For the first time since he was five years old, he heard nothing.

One

SPRAWLED ON THE floor of the backstage area of the Fashion for Fibromyalgia event organized by the Society of Dodge Cove Matrons, Natasha concentrated on pinning the hem of the blue sequined Dolce & Gabbana gown walking the runway in less than—she glanced up at the clock—fifteen minutes. The air smelled faintly of hair spray and expensive perfume. The combination made her nose wrinkle and her eyes water.

"Don't move," she muttered over the pins between her teeth.

"I'm in love with this dress," the cheerleader said, standing on the pedestal in front of a mirror. "I want this for prom."

"Hmm."

It was hard enough to focus when time wasn't on her side without her model twisting around for a better view of the back. Comments about how her ass looked in it didn't help either. Add to that the army of people moving as if all at once to finish hair and makeup, dress fitting, and countless other tasks aimed at pulling off the event without a hitch.

"Are you sure—"

"Casey, you can't bid on the dress you're wearing," Natasha interrupted.

"Boo!" The girl pouted.

"Just. One. Last." She tucked the needle into place. "There!"

Both Natasha and the cheerleader breathed a sigh of relief, as if a great weight had been lifted off their shoulders.

"All right. Just don't sit down and you'll be fine," Natasha said, picking herself up off the floor.

Scissors, needles, and extra thread all went into the emergency sewing kit by her bare feet. She took a moment to smooth out the bell skirt of the Kate Spade dress she wore and patted her backside to clear it of any dust that clung to the pink silk fabric, hoping nothing had stained back there. Then she slipped on her nude pumps, feeling inches taller once more.

The cheerleader stepped down from the platform and teetered away. Not a thank-you. Not even a look back. Figured. Yet Natasha envied the girl. For that night she was a model walking the runway in a beautiful dress. What was Natasha?

Pushing the unbelievably frightening question aside, Natasha turned around and headed for the exit. On the way, she paused at every dressing station, making sure all the models were ready. She might not be participating in the event like her mother wanted her to, but it didn't mean she couldn't help out a little. No other dresses needed pinning, which was good. There was no time for big fixes, but the one-of-a-kind gowns needed to look perfect so the bids went up. The higher the better. The biddies, matrons, and debutantes were always more generous when it was for charity.

When she reached the last dressing stall, one of the assistants was in the process of helping the model out of a blush-toned Armani Privé gown. The fabric sparkled as if a million crystals had been hand-sewn on.

"The show is about to start," Natasha said, pausing in her stride to the exit.

"Tash, one of the matrons reserved this gown," the assistant replied, looking frazzled as she returned the garment into its bag.

Natasha took a deep, calming breath. "And who reserved this gown?"

"Mrs. Vanderlin," the model chimed in.

Feeling the blood rush to her head, Natasha pointed at the gown. "No reservations."

"But—"

"I will take care of Mrs. Vanderlin," another, more subdued voice than Natasha's said from behind her. "Dress her quickly. That gown needs to walk the runway. If Mrs. Vanderlin wants it, then she will have to place a bid like everyone else."

The model quickly hopped into the gown the assistant removed from the dress bag once more.

Natasha bit down on the side of her cheek to keep from wincing. She was supposed to fly under the radar. The last thing she wanted was to be spotted by one of the most important people who helped organize the event. It was wrong of her to think she could escape without notice.

Forcing a smile on her face, Natasha turned around. "Adeline."

The current president of the Dodge Cove Debutante Society returned her smile. They exchanged air kisses on each cheek. Adeline smelled of lilacs.

"I thought you were sitting this one out," Adeline said. Radiant. Calm. Her cascade of dark chocolate hair was tamed into an elegant side-braid. The cream dress she wore had a fifties vibe to it that was both understated and eye-catching.

"Just passing by," Natasha said cordially. "It was on the way. Shouldn't you be in your seat? The show is about to start."

"You know me. I can't sit still for five minutes." She waved a dismissive hand. "Are you sure you can't stay?"

A sheepish grin curled Natasha's lips upward. "Be glad, because I had my eye on that purple Gucci number."

"The one with the feathers?"

Natasha nodded.

Adeline faked concern and teased, "Then you'd best be on your way."

"Oh, don't tempt me," Natasha threatened. "If it wasn't for my appointment, I would totally have a paddle in my hand right now."

The lie flowed out of her lips like honey. There was no appointment that couldn't be rescheduled.

"How is the gap year coming?"

Natasha had made the decision after returning home from Amsterdam almost seven months ago. It was already mid-April and yet the dreaded question that had followed her around still sent chills down her spine. Couldn't people move on? Let go? It was tiring clinging to her ready answer: "It's going really well. Thank you for asking."

Adeline tilted her head as if unconvinced. "Are you sure

you don't want to replace me for the DoCo Debutante Society presidency? You're my first choice."

"I . . . um . . ." Natasha channeled her inner debutante and relaxed her face. Then she glanced at the clock over her shoulder. "I really have to go, Adeline. You know how appointments are." She slowly started backing away.

"Will I see you at the party?" Adeline called after her.

"With bells on!"

Natasha turned on her heel and grabbed her purse and coat from the closet by the exit. Not bothering with buttoning the coat she shrugged on, she pressed against the bar across the door and exited. Once outside she breathed in deeply—the air was so much fresher. It was like drinking a cool glass of water on a hot day. The relief it brought was sublime.

On the way to the white Tesla SUV she'd parked out back, her phone pinged, signaling a new message. The moment she saw the name of the sender she deleted the text, not bothering to read it. She got into her car, slid her phone into the special attachment on the dash, and with the press of a button, started the engine. After buckling in, she checked all mirrors before driving out of the parking lot onto the open road.

Minutes into the drive, Natasha's phone rang. Her first instinct was to ignore the call. But when she read the name on the display, she pulled the hybrid onto the side of the road.

"Hey, baby bro," she said once her twin's handsome face filled the screen.

Nathan's expression soured almost immediately. "I thought we were done with you calling me that."

"Last I heard, you're still two minutes younger than me," she teased.

"Are you in the car?" he asked. "Did I catch you at a bad time?"

"Just finished with my daughterly duties."

"Are you telling me you're not attending the actual event again? Mom's not going to like that."

She hated the admonition in his voice, but what she hated more was the fact that she was running away. Bidding on beautiful dresses would have been fine if not for the questions that came with mingling. What are your plans? Are you interested in an internship? What college are you applying to? Natasha had no answers for any of them.

Sighing, she said, "Adeline actually asked me to be president of the debutantes."

"That's great!" Nathan beamed. "You've wanted that position since you learned what a debutante was."

"Not anymore," Natasha said, feeling nauseous.

"Oh, Tash. Don't be that way."

"What way?"

"Like things are never going to get better." Genuine sadness formed on Nathan's face.

She thumped the back of her head against the seat. "You have your party-planning business. Preston is training to be an Olympian. Caleb, of all people, is in college. And Didi is a brilliant artist. I am nothing."

"Stop that right now. You are not nothing."

"Easy for you to say."

Nathan ran a hand down his face before tapping his chin with a finger. "There's something you can do for me."

"Please don't make me repeat another mantra, because I've heard them all. Mostly from you."

"I am not that bad, am I?" He raised an eyebrow. "And that's not what I meant."

"All right," she said with an exasperated sigh. "Anything for you."

"Will you pick up Didi? She needs a ride to her meeting with Cynthia."

She glanced at her phone. "She should have called me."

"It must have slipped her mind. You know how she gets when she's finishing a painting. And Caleb has class until six."

"I'm on it." Natasha sat up straighter. Despite her ongoing pity party, there was nothing she wouldn't do for her friends and family. Driving Didi to the gallery was easy.

"Good." He smiled. "By the way, I called to let you know our flight is booked."

Natasha bounced in her seat. "You're coming home!"

"Last I heard, we are all invited to the engagement party that will kick off the wedding of the century. So, yes, I'm coming home." Nathan winked. "I wouldn't miss an event planned by Patricia Sinclair."

"You know what they say about meeting your heroes."

"Don't you dare jinx this for me! I'm nervous enough as it is."

"I miss you, little bro."

"Miss you more. And stop calling me that!" Nathan blew her a kiss. "I'll see you soon."

Half an hour later, Natasha parked the Tesla at the curb, got out, and walked up to the door of Didi's house. A fresh coat of paint livened up the once-dull exterior. The yard had yellow spots in places, but the grass was cut and free of litter.

She rang the doorbell and waited. No answer. Natasha shifted to her toes and patted for the Hide-a-Key box on the frame. She slipped the key out of the small rectangular box and let herself in.

Closing the door behind her, she called out, "Didi?"

She went straight toward the kitchen and turned left to Didi's studio. As Nathan had suspected, the artist was seated on a stool in her paint-splattered overalls, chewing on the end of a paintbrush. Two other paintbrushes kept her brown hair in a knot behind her head.

"You're not ready." Natasha stepped forward.

Didi's studio was a small room that perpetually smelled of paint and turpentine, with a wall made entirely of glass that let in natural light. Canvases rested three deep against the other walls, and prints from famous artists Didi loved hung above them.

Seemingly in her own world, Caleb's girlfriend dipped the business end of the brush into a blob of black paint on the palette balanced on her left hand and with expert strokes added shadow to the corner of the canvas before her. From the looks of it, the painting was of an elderly couple holding hands while sitting on a park bench. The image reminded Natasha of something. A memory, maybe. It caused an ache in her chest.

Clearing her throat to ease the growing tightness there, she called Didi's name again. Only louder.

"Natasha!" Didi cried out. She set her painting tools aside and hopped out of her seat, heading straight for Natasha and giving her a big hug. Natasha hoped none of the paint on Didi's overalls was still wet. "You came."

"Of course I came! When Nathan said you needed help, I drove right over. Why didn't you just ask me for help yourself?"

"You've already done so much," Didi said, looking embarrassed. "I never could have gotten that appointment without you. Let me show you what I've done so far."

Didi lifted the still-wet painting off the easel gingerly and placed it against the glass wall. Then she picked up the one Natasha had posed for and rested it on the vacant easel.

Natasha bent forward as close as she could get without pressing her nose against the canvas. The painting featured her in the flapper dress she'd worn for Caleb's Roaring Twenties birthday party. She clutched a strand of pearls in one hand while resting her elbow on her other hand. There was a pensive look on her face. Her hair was gathered to one side and pinned down by a collection of peacock feathers.

The brushstrokes were so fine. And the colors were vibrant. It was as if Natasha was looking at a photo of herself instead of a portrait done in oil. The most amazing part was the backdrop. Instead of being at the party, Natasha found herself in the middle of a crowded street, the only one in period costume.

"Didi, it's gorgeous," Natasha said in awe.

"I'm happy I finished it in time," Didi said, stuffing her hands into the pockets of her overalls. "It's the centerpiece of the collection. I call it *Timeless Princess*."

"I don't know what to say." Natasha's cheeks flamed.

"You don't like it."

"No!" She waved her hands. "It's beautiful. I don't think I ever thought of myself like this."

"Are you kidding me?" Didi gestured at the painting. "You're the perfect muse. Well . . . not as perfect as Caleb, but close."

"That's certainly an ego boost if I ever heard one." She pulled Didi into another tight hug. "Thank you for letting me be a part of this."

"Enough with the mush." Didi stepped back. "Let's head to the gallery before I miss that meeting."

"Maybe we can consider an outfit change first?" Natasha smiled. She strode out of Didi's studio and straight into her room.

"Can't I just go as I am? I mean, my clothes already scream artist," Didi said, following after her.

Natasha narrowed her eyes at Didi.

"I know that look." Didi's eyebrow twitched. "Fine."

"I knew you'd see it my way." Natasha flung open the closet doors and began pushing hangers along the metal bar, one after another.

"It's like Nathan's in the room, except in a dress."

"Ha!" Natasha's lips quirked. "He's an amateur compared to me."

As she pulled out one dress after another, discarding each as soon as she put it against Didi, an unexpected pang of longing hit Natasha so hard it surprised her that she was still standing instead of crumpling into a sobbing ball on the floor.

"What's wrong?" Didi asked.

"It's nothing." Natasha turned back to the closet, embarrassed by the sting in the corner of her eyes.

"Come on. I know it's not."

"It's just . . ." She paused, biting her lower lip. "I remember the days when picking out what to wear was exciting. That feeling of finding the perfect outfit for a date."

"Oh." Didi shifted her weight from one flip-flop to the other. "You mean Jackson."

"I'm being silly."

"No. No, you're not. I'd be a total basket case if Caleb did to me what that jerk did to you."

Drawing on the anger that Didi's words triggered, Natasha inhaled sharply. "I hate his guts and nothing will ever change that. I choose what I wear for myself now and no one else."

"That's the spirit!"

Pressing her lips together to keep them from wobbling, Natasha nodded. "Now, let's get you dressed for that meeting."

Natasha took a deep breath as she sat in her car outside the Cove Gallery, located in downtown Dodge Cove. Many artists who debuted at the Cove—as the locals called it—went on to show in all the top galleries in the world. Its owner and curator possessed one of the best eyes in the business for spotting undiscovered talent.

"Are you sure about this?" Didi asked from the passenger seat as she gazed at the window display. It was the third time she'd asked in the last five minutes. "I mean, it's *the Cove*. I used to stand outside, thinking I was never good enough to go inside."

"Well, now you are going inside, and not only will you wow Cynthia, you will secure your first showing," Natasha said.

"You think so?"

"I know so."

Didi unsnapped her seat belt. Natasha reached over to unsnap her own, but her hand paused at the clasp.

"What's wrong?" Didi asked.

Natasha worried her lower lip again. It had become a habit she didn't like. Yet it always happened when she found herself unsure of what to do. Cynthia was inside the gallery. The gallery owner and Natasha's mother walked in the same circles.

There was no such thing as a secret in Dodge Cove, especially when the talk involved a high-profile debutante. Natasha still hadn't recovered fully from the barrage of questions Adeline had hurled her way. She hated lying. But it was worse to have to admit to the world and to herself that she had no idea what she was doing next.

"Is it okay if I stay here?" Natasha blurted out the question. She twisted around to face Didi. "I mean . . . if you really need me in there, I'll be out of this car in three seconds flat."

Natasha wanted to close her eyes against the hurt she was sure would form on Didi's pretty face. But before she could give in to the urge, Didi took both of Natasha's hands in hers and squeezed them.

"Tash, I can do this." Didi's smile was so bright, it was blinding. "Thank you for driving me here."

"Are you sure?"

Determination hardened her features. "If I can't do this on my own, then I don't have the right to show in that gallery."

A mix of relief and disappointment at herself warred for top position in Natasha's chest. A part of her was happy she could hide away. The other part of her was frustrated that she couldn't even find it in herself to be there for her friend because the urge to avoid questions flung at her was paralyzing.

"I'll be right back," Didi said, pulling Natasha away from her thoughts. She got out of the car and strode confidently into the gallery in the dark jeans, ballet flats, and blazer over a graphic tee that they'd settled on. She looked the part of chic artist ready to conquer the world.

Almost immediately, a powerful sense of abandonment came over Natasha. Everyone was doing their thing. Even the guy she hated the most was living his dream. A year ago, she'd thought she had it all planned. College. The Debutante Society presidency. A solid place in Dodge Cove society. Who knew she would be the one taking the gap year to "find herself"?

Natasha laughed at the imaginary air quotes that popped into her mind.

Not twenty minutes later, Didi was running out of the gallery. She hopped into the passenger seat like a bank robber after a heist and Natasha was her getaway car driver. Didi was breathing hard, a wild look in her eyes. At first, Natasha worried that Didi might be slipping into one of her manic states again. But then she remembered that her friend made sure to take her medication regularly.

"So?" Natasha asked cautiously.

Like she had done earlier, Didi held on to Natasha's hands and squeezed. "I got it!"

It took a second for the words to sink in. Then Natasha said, "You got it!"

They bounced in their seats, squealing like excited girls who'd just been asked by their crushes to attend winter formal. Natasha threw her arms around Didi.

"It was amazing," Didi said. "I strode up to Cynthia and extended my hand."

"Oh, I'm so sorry. I should have told you that Cynthia doesn't do handshakes."

"I got that right away." Didi's beaming smile never lost its luster. "So I launched into talking about how I admired the gallery and about my art. You should have seen her face."

"I'm sure she was impressed."

Didi shook her head. "Actually, she was horrified."

"What?"

"When I told her that I wanted to have a nontraditional show, where the servers dressed like the subjects in the portraits as they mingled with the crowd with trays of drinks and hors d'oeuvres, I thought she was going to faint. All the blood drained from her already-pale face. It was glorious."

"Okay." Natasha inclined her head. "I don't get it. How did she agree to your show?"

"Then I told her about my subjects being prominent residents of Dodge Cove."

"My portrait." Natasha was slowly understanding. Cynthia had never exhibited a show that involved the DoCo elite before. And since Didi had attended so many parties last summer, she'd met enough of them to paint an entire showcase of characters.

"Yes! She said she was intrigued. The show's in three weeks."

"That is fantastic!"

Didi's enthusiasm was catching. It made Natasha feel like she could also do anything if only she put her mind to it.

The question was, what did she want to do?

Two

THE NEXT DAY, in another part of the country, the abrasive metallic *chink* of curtains ripped aside startled Jackson out of a dead sleep. Light pierced through the black comfort of his closed eyelids. He snorted, then groaned, pressing the heel of his hand against his temple as he pushed up and away from the blinding sun.

"What the hell is the matter with you?" came the all-too-familiar bellow of his manager.

Jackson moved his tongue. The dryness of his mouth left a rancid taste. Bile climbed up his throat. He paused in the act of sitting up, waiting. To vomit or not to vomit? That was the question.

"I forgot to take two aspirin with water before I died last night?" Jackson said in response to the question hurled at him.

He finally managed a seated position. One eye opened a slit, allowing him to track the whirlwind of movement that was his manager, who was picking up discarded bottles scattered on the floor and shoving them into a black trash bag. Partying the night before didn't seem like such a good idea in the bright light of day.

After he exhaled long and hard, Jackson said, "Can you call room service and have them bring up some pancakes and lots of bacon? I need to soak up the rest of this booze, man."

Back in Dodge Cove, Jackson and his friends used to party, but never hard enough to pass out afterward. A pang of overwhelming loneliness hit him. He'd thought inviting people over after his gig was the perfect cure. He just didn't want to wind up alone in his too-large suite, faced with the saddest lyrics in the world floating around in his head. He wrote party music for a living, for crying out loud. Unfortunately, the party was over and it left him feeling like roadkill. It was depressing to think that the only person in his life was the man currently tidying up the place.

In the beginning Jackson had felt strong. Independent. Hell, he was going to take over the world. He came close to it too, with a highly successful world tour. Then he saw Natasha again in Amsterdam. Watching her walk away and missing her every day since came crashing into him like a wrecking ball. The party beats were gone and he was afraid he might never get them back.

"I knew you'd forget." Stomping and clomping around like an elephant stampeding followed the hysterical words. "I knew it!"

"Hutch," Jackson barked. "Calm down. It's too early for a tantrum."

The rotund man froze in the act of picking up one of Jackson's discarded shirts and glared at him. "It's already noon, you ungrateful bastard. The rep for Maroon 5 keeps asking for the track you promised for their next album. This new pop star, Crysta Lyn, wants to collab with you after hearing you play last night. And you have the studio booked all afternoon."

Jackson scratched his jaw. The pounding in his head, which he wished he could record because it made one hell of a bassline beat, continued. He still needed hangover food. Badly. And a shower.

Rubbing the last of sleep from his face, forcing his brain to focus, he said, "Tell Adam the track isn't ready yet. Who's this Crysta Lyn again? And cancel studio time. I don't feel like making music today."

Hutch's usually ruddy face turned beet red. His second chin jiggled and his lips quivered. Jackson imagined steam coming out of the man's ears.

"No, we are not canceling studio time," his manager said in a surprisingly even tone. He breathed in, eyes closing for a second. "You haven't had a hit in six months. No one is buying sad, sappy songs. You make dance music, damn it!"

Jackson scowled. "That vein on your neck is about to pop. You should really watch your blood pressure."

In response, Hutch grabbed the leather pants hanging from the back of a chair. Along with the shirt in his hand, he threw both garments at Jackson's face. Then he pointed a pudgy finger Jackson's way.

"I want you at the studio in ten minutes," he said, the threat clear in his voice. "Ten minutes, Jackson!" He waddled to the door. "Do you hear me?"

The door slammed shut before Jackson formed a response.

With both eyes open, he took in the full extent of the events from the night before. His hotel suite was in shambles. A bra hung from the back of the couch. Someone had left a shoe. And several empty bags of chips littered the floor. Hutch must have cleared the room of lingering partygoers, because he was the only one left.

One thing was for sure: Housekeeping had their hands full that morning.

This wasn't the life he'd imagined for himself when he left Dodge Cove to pursue a career as a DJ. He was sick and tired of moving from one hotel room to another—the same overpriced minibar, the same generic desk, even the same Bible on the nightstand.

With tired and creaking joints unfit for someone who'd just turned nineteen, Jackson swung his legs over the side of the bed. The second his feet touched the carpet, he stretched. Joints popped back into place. Then he looked down. Still in the jeans and underwear he'd worn the day before.

Scratching his bare chest, he ambled to the bathroom. The phrase "tired to the bone" had meant nothing to Jackson until that morning. Hutch worked him like a mule. The gigs never stopped. It seemed like a high-class problem to have. He should be happy that people wanted him headlining their clubs and playing their parties. But he wasn't. Not anymore. His feet dragged. His shoulders drooped. Every muscle in his body seemed to have turned to lead overnight.

The wince that came when he stared at his reflection in the mirror was unstoppable. His dyed black hair hung limply to one side. He picked up the electric razor and began shaving the sides and back of his head. The top he kept long and usually slicked back with gel. Then he moved the razor along his chin and jaw.

The purple splotches beneath his eyes were unmistakable. His shoulders and collarbones protruded. Where once he'd had definition and muscle, six months later he was little more than skin and bones. Sleeping all day and working all night did that. He couldn't remember the last time he had hit the gym. If he wasn't in a club or party DJ'ing, he was on a plane or in the studio. The cycle was just too much.

Once he was done shaving, he put down the razor and lifted the tap.

Twenty minutes later, in the shirt and leather pants Hutch had thrown at him, Jackson sat in the studio across the street from his hotel and stared at his phone. A name and a number stared back. His thumb hovered over the Call button.

The producer, who sat beside him in front of a massive soundboard filled with faders, knobs, and buttons, gave him the side eye. Jackson returned the glance with a scowl before he stood up and hit Call.

The number rang a couple of times before it went to voice mail.

Jackson waited for the beep, then said, "Hey, Tash, it's me . . . again. Um, okay, I know I messed up." He ran a hand over the top of his head, smoothing back the gelled strands. "I know I'm the last person you want to talk to, but if you can please return my messages . . ." Then he bowed his head and sighed. "I miss you. I really—"

Another beep cut him off. He ended the call and stared at the screen again. A snort came from behind him.

"Pathetic, man," the producer said. "You can have any girl you want any night of the week and you're begging some girl from home to call you back?"

Turning around, Jackson narrowed his eyes at the guy. "Instead of pissing me off, why don't we just get back to work?"

"Yeah, that's what you said the last hundred times."

Jackson put on his headphones and played the track he had been working on for months. Instantly he was transported to an afternoon by the lake. The sunset colored the placid water bright orange and gold. He was lying on a picnic blanket, his head pillowed by his crossed arms. A yard away, in the water, stood Natasha. She wore a pretty sundress that showed off her shoulders, and she had her hair down.

Nothing else in his life was as beautiful as her.

"Come here," she said, waving him over. "The water is nice."

He shook his head, smiling. "I'm fine here. Thanks."

Who wanted to move when gazing at a view like her was better?

She pouted. "You're no fun."

Powerless against her, he pushed up from the blanket, toed off his boots, and removed his socks. Then he folded up his pant legs and ran toward her. Once his feet were submerged, he bent down and splashed her with water. She shrieked and danced away, laughing even more.

"Bet you regret calling me now, huh?" Jackson challenged.

"Is that the best you can do?"

Never one to walk away from a dare, he charged Natasha. Once she was in his arms, he dove into the water backward, taking her with him. They were soaked and laughing in seconds, tangled in each other's arms. Kissing wasn't too far behind.

"Do you love me?" she whispered when they were back on the blanket, drying off.

"You don't know by now?"

There was that pout again.

Jackson took her hand and placed it at the center of his chest. "Do you feel that?"

She nodded, watching him with clear blue eyes.

"You are every beat of my heart," he said.

Hours later, Jackson threw the headphones against the soundboard and covered his face with his hands. It wasn't working. No matter how hard he tried, the song just wasn't coming together the way he liked. The notes still sounded too depressing. No one wanted to dance to a sad song.

"Fuck," he said into his hands.

"Maybe we should take a break," the producer said.

Jackson knew a break wouldn't help. Not when six months of nothing but crap was coming out of him. The beats used to come easily. He knew how each song would sound way before he laid down tracks. The producer swiveled his chair to face Jackson.

"What if we—"

"We already tried that," Jackson cut off the producer way before the guy finished his thought.

"We can always return to—"

"That version was crap too."

"Okay, looks like you're going to interrupt me any chance you get." The sound of a chair being pushed back followed his words. "I'm going to grab a coffee. Hutch said a song needs to come out of this session or we're not leaving the studio."

Jackson didn't lift his head from his hands until the door of the studio closed. The hourly rate for a studio was astronomical. If he didn't come up with something, they were just wasting money. It wasn't the pressure that bothered him. He had produced something under more stressful conditions. It was that every time he tried to write something new, Natasha's face popped into his mind, influencing the sound of the track. Now all his songs were about missing her. Or not having her in his life. Or wanting her back. These would be all well and good if he were a country artist. But as a dance-party DJ? Not so much.

Unable to stand himself anymore, he picked up his phone and quickly typed a message to the one friend he had left.

JACKSON: Have you heard from Tash lately?

The reply came seconds later.

PRESTON: Hello to you too.
JACKSON: She's not answering any of my calls.
PRESTON: Can you blame her?
JACKSON: I thought when she came to Amsterdam
that everything was going to be okay.
PRESTON: It's never that easy. You know that.
JACKSON: I messed up, man.

He leaned forward until his elbows rested on his knees and cradled his forehead in his free hand. There was a long pause before the next reply came.

PRESTON: Suck it up.

JACKSON: What?

PRESTON: Stop moping and do something about it.

JACKSON: Do you honestly think she'll want to see me when she doesn't even return my calls?

PRESTON: Then make her see you.

JACKSON: Easy for you to say.

PRESTON: Grow a spine. BTW, your brother got engaged.

Jackson almost dropped his phone after reading the text. How come it was the first time he was hearing about it? His thumbs flew over the keypad.

JACKSON: Baxter's engaged? To who?

PRESTON: That's not the point. There's an engagement party. Natasha will be there. Do I have to explain the rest to you or are you smart enough to figure shit out on your own?

JACKSON: When?

PRESTON: Tomorrow.

Jackson pushed to his feet and tucked his phone into his pocket. Quickly, he stuffed all his gear into his pack and left the studio. He had to see her. Had to talk to her in person. Preston was right. There was a quote in his head about a mountain and a guy named Muhammad.

This time, he wasn't allowing her to walk away.

"Where are you going?" the producer asked when they passed each other in the hallway.

"Back to the hotel," Jackson said over his shoulder, not once stopping.

After jogging across the street, he slipped into the lobby of his hotel, ignoring the cheerful greeting of the night manager. He pressed the triangle pointing up and seconds later the elevator doors parted, letting him in. Finding his floor number, he punched the button.

His phone vibrated.

Thinking it was another text from Preston, Jackson slipped the device out of his back pocket only to realize it was a call. From Hutch.

"Where the hell did you go?" bellowed his manager. "You have a gig at Velvet tonight."

"Have someone fill in for me," Jackson said as he slid the keycard into the slot and pushed into his hotel room.

All signs of the party from the previous night were gone. He ended the call before Hutch could yell at him some more. Dumping his pack onto the bed, he opened the airline app on his phone and quickly typed in the destination. There was a red-eye leaving in two hours.

With a tap of his finger, he booked the ticket. His phone rang again. He checked and ignored Hutch's call. He pulled his duffel out of the closet and quickly stuffed clothes into it, not bothering to fold them. Then he called the front desk for a cab.

He had a plane to catch.

Jackson Mallory was going home.

Three

THE ENGAGEMENT PARTY for Baxter and Adeline was kicked off by cocktails at the lesser ballroom of Mallory Manor before dinner on Friday. Natasha greeted the happily engaged couple at the door and handed over the flowers she'd brought for Adeline. Even if guests had been asked to make charitable donations instead of bringing gifts, she couldn't come empty-handed.

Natasha had always loved the lesser ballroom. Its floor area opened out onto the expansive patio overlooking the grounds. Something that the grand ballroom didn't have, since it was on the second floor of the property. People were already outside, enjoying the mild early evening weather. She admired the standing tables added to the room for those who wanted to have a place to set their drinks down. The floral centerpieces were beautiful, made up of white peonies, the future bride's favorite flower. Natasha sighed. Everything was too beautiful for words.

Supporting an elbow with one hand and holding a glass of ginger ale with the other, Natasha pretended to ignore the fact that she was standing in a room where she and Jackson used to make out.

A lot.

In fact, in her periphery, she spotted the heavy curtains he'd loved to pull her behind.

Every time there was a party at a manor, she and Jackson always found a way to sneak off. Her chest felt tight at the memory of his smile and the way he ran his thumb over her lips before he kissed her. It was a bad idea to come here. She knew the Ghosts of Relationship Past would come back and haunt her the second she stepped into his house. But she had promised to attend. And Natasha liked Baxter. She couldn't let her heartbreak get in the way of showing her support for his engagement to Adeline. She was happy for them. She really was. They had what she'd once had. Now, if she could only survive the night without breaking down, she'd call it a win.

Plus, her periwinkle silk charmeuse Valentino with beading made her feel pretty, confident—like a girl who wasn't lost and heartbroken. She loved how the fabric moved when she did— lighter than air. The hem of the full skirt fell a few inches above her knee and the bodice was cinched in at the waist. Her one regret was the new Jimmy Choos on her feet. Breaking them in at a party where lots of standing around was involved was a rookie move on her part. In her defense, they'd looked so sexy in the store that she just had to have them.

"Isn't this just marvelous?" Nathan bumped his shoulder

against hers. He held a pretty green mocktail while grinning like a kid in a candy store.

Distracted from her aching toes, Natasha hugged him for the hundredth time since he'd arrived with Preston the day before. It was so nice to have her twin back.

"Have I told you how much I've missed you?"

He counted off with his fingers as he spoke. "Um . . . when I was packing for this trip. When I was on my way to the airport. While I was settling in on the plane. Shortly after onboard Wi-Fi was activated. When we landed—"

Her laughter cut him off. "I get it. But I really did miss you. Why did you have to move all the way to Colorado?"

In unison, their eyes landed on the tall, built-like-a-Greek-god guy who was laughing at something Caleb had said. Or he might have been laughing at Didi, who stood beside him in the pale pink dress Natasha had helped her pick out for the party.

"I still can't believe he shaved his head. It's so sexy," she said with a sigh.

"Stop drooling over my boyfriend, please. Or hair extensions will come off," he snapped back. "But I also completely understand where the worship is coming from. He *does* fill that sports jacket with deliciousness."

"How does it feel?"

Nathan's eyebrows knitted together. "What?"

"Finally getting to call him your boyfriend."

"Oh, stop it!"

"Come on. Tell me."

He rolled his eyes and smiled. "Some days I wake up and think it's all a dream. Then he smiles at me, and I know it's all real."

As if sensing that Natasha and Nathan were both staring at him, Preston glanced their way. Almost immediately his expression changed from passive to adoring. Those green eyes focused on Nathan like he was the only person there. Like Nathan belonged to no one else. He smiled and turned his attention back to Caleb and Didi. For a moment, Natasha saw someone other than Preston staring back. That was exactly the way Jackson used to look at her. Like she was his whole world. Her feet seemed unsteady all of a sudden, like she'd broken a heel and was about to topple over.

Blinking the image of Jackson away, she steadied herself and focused on what was really important: teasing Nathan.

She poked her twin in the arm repeatedly. "How are you still standing right now?"

"I'm hiding it well, but my knees are Jell-O." Nathan inhaled sharply. "Isn't this party just perfect? Everything is within the blue, green, and ivory color scheme that I'm already suspecting are the colors of the wedding. White peonies everywhere. And the food and drinks are impeccable. I didn't expect any less."

Her brother's fledgling party-planning business was gaining a reputation for excellence, especially with Eleanor Grant's recommendation after he had put together the Society of Dodge Cove Matrons luncheon back in October. Natasha was so proud of him. She envied his ability to know what he wanted and go after it with single-minded determination.

She needed a new dream. Something she could call her own. But as soon as the thought entered her mind and she wanted to tell Nathan about it, her brother spotted the party planner and left Natasha to fend for herself. The biddies descended upon her like sharks scenting blood in the water.

Needing a break from all the mingling and the heavy-handed questions about her future, Natasha left the lesser ballroom for the powder room nearby. A minute to herself was all she needed. She pushed open the door and entered. The sounds of sniffling reached her immediately.

"Is everything okay?" Natasha asked as she neared the young woman she recognized as one of the new debutantes sitting on a divan at the center of the small room with her face in her hands.

"He's such a jerk," the girl said, her voice quivering.

Natasha pulled a couple of tissues from the holder by the porcelain sink and handed them over. The debutante took them gratefully and began dabbing at her tearstained face. For a second, Natasha worried for her makeup, but it seemed everything stayed in place, even the mascara on her lashes.

"You're Stacy, right? Stacy Richmond," she said. "You just moved here last year?"

Stacy's eyes grew wide. "You're *the* Natasha Parker."

"I don't know about 'the.'" Natasha's smile wobbled. "Just Natasha is fine. I hope you don't mind my asking." She gestured at Stacy's slightly splotchy complexion. "What happened?"

A new wave of tears gushed from Stacy's eyes, accompanied by the crumpling of her pretty face. Natasha eased closer and rubbed soothing circles down the other girl's back.

It took a couple of minutes, but the keening cries ebbed and Stacy was able to speak again. More tissues were involved. Natasha waited patiently.

Taking a deep, shuddering breath, Stacy said, "He's cheating on me."

The moment the word "cheating" left Stacy's mouth, Natasha

went on the defensive. She understood Stacy's heartbreak. Sisters had to stick together.

"Who?" Natasha racked her brain, but she couldn't come up with the name of the guy Stacy was with. Her debutante gossip wasn't up to date since she'd decided to lie low.

"Peyton."

"McMasters?"

Stacy nodded, seeming like another crying jag was on the way. Finally, a name. Natasha's mind immediately thought of the many ways to make the jerk pay for making such a sweet girl cry. At a party, no less.

"I went to high school with him," Natasha said through tight lips. "He used to be on the lacrosse team. How did you find out that he was cheating on you?"

"Someone sent me a picture, and when I confronted him about it, he broke up with me."

Natasha stood and headed for the door.

"Where are you going?" Stacy asked, still sniffling.

But Natasha didn't reply. Instead she went back into the lesser ballroom and snagged a champagne glass from a passing tray. She gathered as much spit as she could in her mouth, the way Caleb taught her when they were kids, and dropped everything into the glass. Then she lifted her head and scanned the crowd for her target.

Jackson checked his reflection in the mirror one more time, adjusting the tie around his neck. It felt too tight. He loosened the knot and started over. About halfway through, he pulled the tie off and flung it over the back of a nearby chair. Wearing it felt like having a noose around his neck. He unbuttoned the top of his shirt and tugged the cuffs out from the ends of the sleeves of his dinner jacket.

It had been a while since he'd had to dress in something other than jeans and a T-shirt. The starch the household staff used when ironing his clothes made his skin itch. Coming home to Natasha had fueled him on the plane ride over, but the second he stepped over the town line he began questioning himself. Was he doing the right thing by coming back? He knew he needed Natasha in his life. But what if she never took him back? What if she moved on?

The last question practically crippled him. He had to see her. But seeing her also meant seeing his family. Sneaking into the house was easy enough because of its size. Yet the second he attended the party, they would all know he was back.

He turned his head left, then right. The sides were starting to grow out. His hair always started darker, then lightened as the strands grew longer. He considered shaving off the top after his shower but decided against it. Might be too severe a look for his first party in town. So he worked a glob of gel into the strands and combed everything back.

He sighed and then gave himself a stern look in the mirror. "You can do this."

Then he walked out of his room and into the hall. Unfortunately, his confidence wavered the closer he got to the lesser ballroom. And it was a long trip. He had to traverse the grand staircase to the foyer, take a right into the music room, move across the sunroom, and then take a left past the center atrium with its glass dome and hothouse flowers.

The guests he passed stopped and stared. He nodded and smiled, keeping his pace even. The whispering started as soon as he passed. No one even bothered waiting for him to be out of earshot.

"Here we go," he said under his breath.

Just at the entrance stood Baxter and Adeline, looking like the handsome power couple they were.

Baxter froze in the middle of greeting the Feldsteins. He even had Dr. Feldstein's hand in his. Adeline noticed the sudden change in Baxter and followed his gaze. Like a pro, she thanked the Feldsteins and gestured for them to enter the ballroom. Then she wrapped her arm around Baxter's and gave him a squeeze.

Jackson cleared his throat and forced himself to move the five steps it took to be standing in front of the couple. The tips of his fingers tingled. And sweat drenched his pits. *Thank God for jackets*, he thought. No one had to know how nervous he was.

"Hey, Bax," he said, not quite making eye contact with his brother, who was twelve years his senior.

"You're here," Baxter said, surprise and shock crossing his face one after the other. "When did you get back?"

"Couple hours ago."

"Welcome home," Adeline said, warmth in her voice. "We're so glad you came to the party."

"I never got the invitation," Jackson replied. "There must have been some mix-up in the mail since I move a lot. If not RSVP'ing is an issue, I can leave—"

"No!" Baxter said, cutting him off. Then he pulled Jackson into a tight, brotherly embrace. "You're actually here."

"Yeah." Jackson clapped his brother's back. "Congratulations, dude."

"Jackie," his mother said from behind Baxter and Adeline. "You're home!"

Words died when Jackson's gaze landed on his father, who stood at his mother's side. The white on the man's temples wasn't there a year ago. Neither were the harsh lines bracketing his lips. Yet his eyes, golden like Jackson's, remained as cold as ever. Even if he was in his midfifties, he stood tall and proud. Spine straight. Expression unforgiving.

"I see the prodigal son has returned," Hayden Mallory said, a glass of scotch in one hand.

"Dad," Jackson said.

"I take it you being here means you're done with this DJ business?"

All eyes were on Jackson, but his attempts at a response were choked by the closing walls of his throat.

"Dad, please," Baxter said. "Let's not do this here."

"Hayden, why don't we let Jackson settle in before we start asking him questions," his mother said. "This is not the time or place."

"There is never a good time for this kind of thing, Camilla," his father said. Then he gestured with his glass toward Jackson. "This is what happens when you coddle your son too much. He goes and gets a ridiculous haircut, and runs off doing God knows what, tarnishing the good name of this family. Baxter is a rising star at Parker and Associates and is on track to make partner. After that I have political plans for him. He may even be president one day. Can't you see that?"

His mother touched the pearls around her neck. In her distress, she opened her mouth but no words came out.

"It's okay, Mom." Jackson gave her a sad smile before

turning his attention to Adeline and Baxter. "I'm sure you have many more guests to greet, so I'll excuse myself. Baxter, we'll catch up later."

"We'll do that." Baxter gave him a subtle nod.

Not making eye contact with anyone for fear of saying something he might regret, Jackson turned on his heel and headed into the ballroom. His father's words were like a physical blow. They hurt and would definitely leave bruises in the morning. He'd never understood Jackson's decision to become a DJ, so some pushback was expected. But his disapproval wasn't welcome, especially when Jackson was struggling with his music. It sucked and it pissed him off. So with his head down, he kept moving, as far away from his father's judgment as possible.

Not paying attention to where he was going, he bumped into someone crossing his path. There was a *splat*. A feminine gasp reached his ears as the glass of champagne in her hand spilled all over the front of her dress. Jackson reached out as if to catch her, an apology already on his lips. Then their eyes met and the clear blue that stared back—despite the annoyance in them—took Jackson's breath away.

Four

HER DRESS. THE beautiful dress she'd been so excited to wear that evening was completely ruined. Her spit-laced champagne dripped all over the front to the floor. Anger rose from the pads of Natasha's feet up her body like a kettle about to blow. The words "Watch it, jerk!" were about to fall out of her mouth when she remembered where she was.

Even in public, she could still hiss and throw death-dagger eyes at whoever had the nerve not to pay attention to where he was going. No one ruined a Valentino and got away with it. Not on her watch. Natasha lifted her narrowed gaze to the person who'd bumped into her, ready to lay down the hurt.

Time stopped.

Her heart punched against the wall of her chest. Hard.

All the blood in her body froze.

Jackson. Was in Dodge Cove. Jackson was in Dodge Cove and he had black hair. He had black hair?

"What are you doing here?" she blurted out.

"Why haven't you been answering my calls or returning my texts?" he replied.

Her first instinct was to turn around and storm away. It had worked the last time they'd spoken. But they were attracting too much attention already with the spilling-of-the-champagne incident. The last thing Baxter and Adeline needed at their engagement party was to have the night ruined because of a scene she and Jackson caused.

Some reunion it was. Not in her wildest dreams had she expected him to actually come back. Seeing him again brought out a whirl of conflicting emotions. She was mad that he had the gall to show his face in Dodge Cove again. That stupid, handsome-as-sin face. She didn't know if she wanted to laugh or cry. And damn if the sound of his voice didn't make her insides pay attention. Even after all the pain he had caused her, she still felt the magnetic pull he always seemed to have on her. Well, not anymore, damn it! Jackson being back changed nothing.

Except that his presence made it seem like all ears were aimed in their direction, waiting for the juiciest piece of gossip. Or, better yet, the next DoCo scandal. Jackson and Natasha together again—what could go wrong? Other than everything.

"We are not doing this here," she said.

"The terrace, then."

Attempting to regain some control, she deposited the empty flute on a passing tray. She didn't bother looking back to see if Jackson followed when she headed outside. The prickle running along her back told her so. She could actually feel him staring at her like she had a bull's-eye painted somewhere on her backside.

Thankfully, most of the guests had moved inside, so they wouldn't have too many witnesses for whatever came next. Natasha went straight to the farthest corner of the terrace and whirled around. The slight chill in the air made her very aware of the wet condition of her dress and how thin the fabric was. She crossed her arms and scowled.

There were many nights when she'd had dreams of confronting him again after Amsterdam. In those dreams, she felt brave and always had the right thing to say—just like in Amsterdam. Yet no matter how hard she tried, all her confidence ebbed away, leaving a big, gaping, Jackson-shaped hole. Twelve months of patching up that hole left her cold and miserable inside.

How could she ever repair the damage of losing a soul mate? Because that was what he was to her. At least at the time she'd thought so.

Now there he stood in front of her, so tall, so unbelievably, frustratingly good-looking. It pissed her off even more. Natasha hugged herself tighter in the hopes of squeezing the unwanted feelings out of her. Where had the calm and collected Natasha gone?

Jackson shrugged out of his jacket and made a move to drape it over her shoulders. Natasha stepped back. He gave her that exasperated look that never failed to make her weak in the knees.

"How dare you show your face here?"

"Don't be stubborn, Tash," he said. "I'm the reason why

you're soaked. I wasn't paying attention to where I was going. At least let me give you my jacket before you catch a cold."

She shook her head. "I don't want *anything* from you."

His shoulders sagged, but the jacket stayed in his hand. Not in a million years was she asking for it. Freezing to death was preferable, thank you very much. Okay, maybe a tad over-dramatic, but she had a point to make.

"And what made you think that not replying to your messages and calls meant come home, huh?" she hissed, addressing his earlier question. "I never thought you were the type who couldn't take a hint. We're over, Jackson. Face it."

"Tash, come on." He ran his fingers through his hair. "I messed up. I'm willing to admit that. But please let me explain."

"What else is there to say? You left. Plain and simple." Her glare grew ten degrees hotter. "What can you possibly say that will justify what you did?"

"The moment I signed with Hutch, he wanted me in LA as soon as possible. There was no time—"

"I call bullshit," she barked. "I'm your—" She shut her mouth, then corrected herself. "I *was* your girlfriend. Didn't I at least deserve a call? Maybe even a text? Because here I thought a face-to-face might be asking for too much."

"It's not that simple."

"I think I'm smart enough to understand."

"I knew if you asked me not to go that I'd stay," he whispered, bowing his head and squeezing the back of his neck, remorse on his too-thin face. "But that doesn't matter anymore. I'm back and I'm willing to do anything. I love you, Tash."

"Excuse me? You *love* me? Where the hell was that love the

night you decided to pack up and leave? Huh?" Her earlier anger reignited, and the tinder was indignation.

"Tash—"

"Stop! Just stop!" She raised a hand. "I don't have time for your lies. I'm wet. I'm cold. I have to go."

"Everything okay here?" Caleb asked.

Jackson ran a hand down his face as Natasha looked over his shoulder at the new arrivals. Caleb, Didi, Nathan, and Preston all stood a couple of yards away, wearing different expressions. Her brother seethed and seemed close to cutting someone. Caleb seemed uncertain, stuffing his hands in his pockets. Preston remained stone-faced, making him hard to read. And Didi . . . Well, she was more than mildly curious. In fact, she was the first to break ranks.

"So, you're *the* Jackson everyone loves to hate," Didi said, circling him like a shark and giving him a once-over. Jackson followed her with his gaze. "I thought you were blond. Isn't he supposed to be blond?" She addressed that question to Natasha.

"I dyed my hair," Jackson said.

"Didi, get away from him," Nathan said, as if Jackson were a mangy dog.

Didi stepped back, but instead of returning to Caleb's side, she stood beside Natasha, entwining their arms. Natasha took immense comfort not only in the body heat Didi provided but also in the support. Unfortunately, the comfort sucked out all her previous indignation, leaving her tired and miserable. All feeling from the waist down vanished. She barely understood how she remained upright when curling into a ball was preferable. They said mourning a breakup took twice as long as the actual relationship. If that were true, then how was Natasha supposed to recover from someone she'd loved since she was six years old?

Seeing Jackson in Dodge Cove felt like seeing a ghost. She wasn't sure if he was real or a figment of her active imagination. Yet the rational part of her brain knew better. There was no such thing as ghosts.

"Let's go home and get you out of that dress," Nathan finally said, barely keeping his cool. His lips quivered and his eyebrow twitched. A vein pulsed in his temple.

Natasha knew what they were all not saying . . . or in their case, not doing. A room away was the entire DoCo elite. Raised voices attracted unwanted attention. But it was becoming increasingly clear that Jackson and Natasha were a powder keg waiting to blow.

Cold and in shock, Natasha tightened her grip on Didi and forced herself to move.

"Tash, please." Jackson moved toward her but Nathan was already there, putting a hand on his chest and hissing into his ear.

"I'd stay where you are if you know what's good for you."

Jackson met Nathan's gaze. Then, face falling, he raised both hands and backed away a step.

"Nathan," Preston said. "Let's go."

"You better not show yourself to me when there's no one around," Nathan said, his parting shot before he followed the rest of them out.

During the plane ride home, Jackson had rehearsed everything he wanted to say. He was confident. Cocky even. Yet the second he'd seen the hurt in Natasha's eyes, he'd choked. A year ago he would have beaten anyone who made her sad. How fucked up was it that he had been the one to ultimately shatter the girl he loved?

Head in his hands as he sat in one of the chairs in the smaller of the two libraries, Jackson hated himself for hurting her. She deserved better, he knew that now. But he wasn't going to walk away. Not until she and everyone else forgave him for being the shittiest person alive.

He looked up at the cuckoo clock hanging on the wall. It was in the shape of a house with flowers painted on the front paneling. The roof created the perfect letter A.

Above the clock face was a balcony with two doors. What had always fascinated Jackson most about the clock was the sound it made. When the long hand reached the top, the double doors swung open, revealing a woman holding a bird. It cuckooed to the number where the small hand pointed.

This clock had started Jackson's fascination with sound. He heard the music of things. The humming of the fridge. The steady chopping of their cook preparing vegetables for dinner. Bees in the woods buzzing around their hive. The tinkling wind chimes on a branch of the massive oak in the garden. And the best sound of all: Natasha's laughter. Nothing could compare to its brightness. To its clarity. When she laughed, it was as if the world was a perfect place.

"I figured you'd be here," came a masculine voice from his left.

Lips pressed together, Jackson sighed. "Didn't you leave with the rest of them?"

Caleb shrugged. "Forgot my jacket."

"And you're looking for it here? Because this is not the coatroom."

"I admire your balls, Mallory," Caleb said, stuffing his hands in his pockets and leaning against the side of one of the shelves. "You're really being sarcastic with me right now? After that shit storm at the patio?"

"I should really be saying, 'Screw you, Parker.'" Jackson paused. "But you're right."

"Excuse me?" Caleb cocked his head. "Can you repeat that? I didn't hear you correctly."

Jackson snorted. "You're right. Cut the sarcasm."

"Maybe there's hope for you yet."

What was Jackson supposed to say to that? He was on the wrong side of things. In fact, Caleb had every right to deck him. But it seemed like Caleb was willing to cut him some slack. Jackson took the chance and ran with it.

"Hey, that thing with Tash earlier . . . ," he began, but a sudden lump in his throat prevented him from continuing.

"To be honest, bro, she was hell to be around for the first two months after you left," Caleb said, a flash of anger in his eyes.

Jackson lifted his head. "What happened?"

"She was a mess." Caleb rubbed his forehead. "She'd cry all night. Sleep all day. No matter how hard we tried, we just couldn't get her to leave her room. Forget showering. I never thought someone that pretty could smell that funky. But that was for the first month."

Jackson hesitated to ask, afraid of the possible answer, but the question fell from his lips anyway. "And the second month?"

Caleb sighed. "That was when the partying started."

"Tash?" His straitlaced, perfect debutante, DoCo princess, a party girl?

"I'm not kidding. If there was a party happening within town limits, she was there. At first, we thought it was a good thing. She was getting out of the house. Interacting with people. Rejoining the world."

"Wait. We're talking about the same girl here, right?"

"You try babysitting her when all she wants is to get drunk. Nathan, Preston, and I had our hands full making sure she stayed out of harm's way. She basically imploded when you left. I'm surprised she managed to pull herself together after that."

"Do you hate me too? For leaving?"

"Jax."

"Because I'm starting to see that there's a pretty long line." Jackson stared at his hands, curling them into tight fists. "I didn't know I hurt so many people, Caleb. I thought I was following my dream and that everyone would be happy for me. I didn't mean to . . ." He swallowed, hard. The corners of his eyes stung. "I'm such a selfish bastard."

A hand rested on his shoulder.

"I'm not going to lie, what you did was a shit move," Caleb said, his tone stern. "But, damn if I don't see where you're coming from. All I ever really wanted was to get out of this town. Even planned an entire gap year around it. But then I met Didi."

The complete adoration in Caleb's face was all too familiar. Jackson looked at Natasha that way. Like his entire world revolved around her.

"I can't say I'm surprised," Jackson said. "But it was just a matter of time. I'm happy you found her, Caleb. I really am."

"More like she found me." Caleb shook his head. "But we're not here to talk about my relationship. I'm assuming the reason you're in Dodge Cove is because you want to make things right with Tash. Because God help you if it's not. I'd be the first to punch your lights out."

"I need her in my life, Caleb." Jackson looked his friend in the eye. "I was wrong to leave without telling her. I was wrong to leave, period."

"You know what they say: Admitting you were wrong is the first step."

"Isn't it supposed to be admitting you have a problem?"

"Are you seriously correcting me right now?"

Jackson lifted both his hands. "You're right."

Caleb studied him. "So how are you going to fix this?"

Jackson stood, then looked up at the cuckoo clock one more time before he turned to leave.

"Where are you going?" Caleb called after him.

"Making things right," he said over his shoulder.

"Then I'm glad you're back."

For the first time since coming home, Jackson smiled genuinely. "Me too."

He left the library and went straight for the manor's front door. Along the way he spotted a large bouquet on a table. It didn't seem like it belonged to anyone. No card. So he grabbed it. He figured where he was headed, flowers could only help.

Five

A YEAR AGO, the Dodge Cove Spring Ball was one of the many important events in Natasha's calendar. All debutantes had to attend it. And with her bid for the presidency of the DoCo Debutante Society officially in full swing, she needed to make a good impression.

As she sat in front of one of the many vanity mirrors in the dressing room, she concentrated on applying the finishing touches to her makeup. Then her gaze landed on her phone. It sat beside all her makeup, not having rung once since she'd started getting ready.

She picked up the phone and unlocked the screen. No message icon. No missed call.

Still, she checked her voice mail.

Seconds later, a voice told her what it had been telling her since she'd arrived at the venue: no new messages. Where could Jackson be? It was unlike him to be late when escorting her during an event. A pang of worry grew in her gut.

As soon as the ball ended, Natasha borrowed Nathan's roadster and drove as fast as the law allowed to Mallory Manor. She didn't bother changing out of her gown. A mix of fear and anger balled in her gut as she jumped out of the car. Jackson's motorcycle wasn't parked where it usually was. But it didn't mean he wasn't home.

Natasha didn't ring the bell. Instead she pushed through the front doors and ran up the curling grand staircase that led to the second floor. Her skirt billowed around her. Wisps of her hair escaped their fastenings. The door to Jackson's room was cracked open when normally it would be shut. She shoved it aside and barreled in.

"Jax!" She looked around, breathing hard.

She let her gaze roam the space. Posters of music festivals filled the walls. An electric guitar and amp sat in a corner. And shelves of vinyl records lined the far end of the room.

The bed had been made. Like it always was. But the top two drawers of the dresser were left open. His leather jacket, which he usually hung over the back of his desk chair, was missing. And the door to his closet was open.

The space smelled so much like him. Masculine yet neither sharp nor spicy. Clean boy. All Jackson.

But something was missing. The air was too still.

Her anger from having been stood up quickly drained out of her, like she had jumped into the lake in winter. It was replaced by an unexplained sense of something not being right. Frigid dread sprang up as cold sweat on her fingertips.

She took a tentative step toward the closet and then another until she reached the door. It had also been left ajar. As if Jackson hadn't bothered closing it. She placed her hand on its wooden surface and nudged it farther in.

Natasha didn't know what she was looking for when she stepped inside. All the suits and formal wear were still hanging in neat rows. The tailcoat he should have worn to the ball had been left untouched on its hanger.

As if a voice told her to turn around, Natasha faced the other side of the closet. The cubbies that held his shirts and jeans were in disarray. Like someone had packed in a hurry.

Heart pounding, she ran out of the closet to his desk. The place where his laptop usually sat was empty.

Now, standing in the shower, Natasha felt as lost as that night. As soon as the hot water hit her head and shoulders, all the pain of being abandoned came flooding back. The emotional wound she thought had scarred over reopened and she was bleeding. She dropped to her knees and covered her face as the tears came streaming down. Her sobs bounced off the tiles. She prayed Didi or Nathan wouldn't hear her, but she was sure that wasn't the case. Even if she insisted she wanted to be alone, they wouldn't leave.

Her heart hurt. If she kept the sobs inside, she was sure her chest would break open. So she cried out like she was dying . . . because she was. Jackson, the once love of her life, was back. There was no unseeing him. And it sucked.

She was Humpty Dumpty. Just when she thought she'd managed to glue back all the pieces, she fell off that wall again. The only difference now was she wasn't afraid to ask Didi and Nathan for help to put her back together again. That had been her mistake the first time around: thinking she could do it all herself. She had friends. She had family. They were ready and willing. It was wrong to suffer alone.

Once the flood of emotions receded and Natasha could stand again, she turned off the water and stepped out of the shower. She didn't bother looking at her reflection in the mirror. It was fogged up anyway. She shrugged on her robe and padded to the door, still dripping.

The second she exited the bathroom, Didi handed her a cool cucumber eye mask. A corner of Natasha's lips turned up. She was right. They had heard her. But she was also right in leaning on them for support.

She took the mask gratefully and put it on. The cool gel inside the soft plastic was a welcome balm to her burning eyes. DoCo debutantes didn't walk around with puffy eyes. That was an unspoken rule.

"Thanks," she mumbled.

"Come over to the bed," Didi said. "I'll dry your hair."

"You don't have to do that." Natasha touched the wet strands.

"But I want to." Didi's firm tone said that was the end of it.

Some of the hurt ebbed away as Natasha watched Didi enter the bathroom. A second later, she came out with a fresh towel in her hands. She pointed at the bed. Natasha sat down on the edge and let Didi get to work.

"Where's Nathan?" Natasha asked, fearing her brother had stormed back to Mallory Manor to teach Jackson a thing or two. A part of her really wanted that to be true. The other part just needed her brother close by.

"He's getting the pizza." Didi squeezed out the excess water from the long, damp strands.

"Extra cheese?"

"You know it."

Warmth eased more of the pain. Her brother knew her well, having gone through the routine once before. Later that night, Natasha wouldn't be surprised to find a pint of pralines and cream and a spoon waiting for her.

"He's back," Natasha said.

"Stating the Obvious for five hundred, Alex," said Didi before handing the towel over to her.

"But he's not supposed to be back. That's the point."

"So that's *your* Jackson, huh?"

Natasha narrowed her eyes at Didi. "He's not *my* Jackson. He's no one's Jackson. At least, not anymore."

"Will you kill me if I say I think his hair is kind of cool? I can't imagine him blond."

"More like golden-haired," Natasha said absentmindedly as she wrapped the towel around her head. "Imagine a lion's mane. You should have seen him in grade school—" She bolted to her feet and paced the length of her room. "No! I am not going down memory lane. I'm too angry."

"Why do you think he's back?"

"Clearly to cause trouble," Nathan said as he entered the room, a large pizza in his hands.

He laid the box on the bed and popped the lid. The smell of cheese and tomato sauce and cooked dough filled the room. Natasha immediately veered toward the pie and separated a slice for herself. The gooey cheese stretched, leaving strings behind. She stuffed the end into her mouth and inhaled a large bite. Despite the hot cheese burning her tongue, her eyes rolled to the back of her head.

"Thank God," she said between chews, covering her mouth with her hand. "I'm starving."

The carbs helped Natasha push back the last of her pain. With Didi and Nathan by her side, she could focus on the most important emotion: anger.

Didi shrugged. "For all you know, he didn't come back here to cause trouble. Maybe he's just stopping by? He was invited to the engagement party, right?"

Nathan put his slice down, wiped his greasy fingers on a napkin, and sat on the side of the bed. He wrapped his arms around Didi and pulled her close until her head rested on his chest. Then he stroked her chin-length brown hair.

"My sweet, innocent Didi. This is why I love you so much," he cooed. "Caleb may be a jerk sometimes, but he's tame compared to Jackson. You don't know him like we do, honey."

Didi hugged him back for a second before pulling away and returning her attention to Natasha.

"What's wrong, Tash?" Didi asked, picking up her pizza again. "Does Jackson being here really bother you that much?"

Natasha blinked. "More than I thought it would. I thought confronting him in Amsterdam was the end, the closure I needed, but seeing him again . . ."

"He looked like a mess," Nathan commented. "Did you see him?"

"You mean that's not how he usually looks?" Didi asked.

"No," Natasha said, pushing away the pang of concern. "He looks really tired."

Nathan shuddered. "Give it a month and he might actually become a ghost."

"Nate!" Natasha's eyes widened. "I may hate the guy's guts,

but I don't want him . . ." She thought about it. "Well, maybe I want him dead. Just a little."

"I really don't get it." Didi pulled a pinch of cheese from the slice in her hand and popped it into her mouth. "He left."

Nathan and Natasha nodded.

"He didn't say anything to anyone about it," Didi continued. "And he broke your heart because of it."

"Where is this going?" asked Natasha. She eased herself onto one corner of the bed and folded her legs in front of her.

"You should have seen Tash back then." Nathan rolled his eyes. "Pints of ice cream in the freezer weren't safe. She even walked around without makeup on. It was horrible."

"Sure, because being brokenhearted is so glamorous," Natasha protested.

"Did you ever consider going after him?" Didi asked, still riding the train of thought she'd climbed on.

The temperature dropped in the room. Both Nathan and Natasha froze.

"What?" Didi looked from one twin to the other. "Did I say something wrong? Because I ran after Caleb when I thought he was still at the airport. And if I could have afforded the ticket to London, I think I would have gone all the way there. Thank God he came back. Saved me the trip."

Tension rose like water filling a tank. No one moved. No one made a move to speak. Lips remained tightly sealed, until the silence got oppressive. Two sets of eyes waited almost unblinking for Natasha's reply.

So she went for the truth. "A guy like that didn't deserve me running after him."

* * *

Flowers in his hand, Jackson stared up at the trellis he had to climb in order to reach the balcony on the second floor of Parker Manor—baby sister to the Parker Estate, their family's ancestral home. It was the fastest route to see Natasha, since climbing up to her balcony had always been his go-to move after curfew. With his luck, the trellis would be rotted through, causing him to fall and break his neck. Ringing the doorbell was the most sensible option. Her mom might let him in. Her dad might not. And Nathan might pull a knife on him. Jackson had to see her, and there were too many obstacles if he used the regular way into the house. So up the trellis it was.

Not that he imagined more than a redo of his first encounter with Natasha post-return to Dodge Cove. Spilling champagne down her dress and enduring toxic glares from his friends wasn't the way to go. For his second attempt at contact, he considered two possible outcomes.

The first was that he and Natasha would sit down and talk. That was the best-case scenario. The dream. Unfortunately, from what Caleb had told him, the universe might be inclined to follow the second, which had several permutations. Many of them ended with his death and dismemberment. He hoped the bouquet he'd brought along would help to soften any blows she aimed his way.

After sending a silent prayer to whoever was listening, Jackson placed the stems of the bouquet between his teeth, grabbed onto the trellis with both hands, and positioned one foot on the first rung. Maybe he should have changed from dress shoes to boots first.

* * *

Tired from the roller coaster of emotions, Natasha sat in front of her vanity mirror, unraveling the towel on her head. She dabbed at the last of the water in her hair and set the towel aside. Then she picked up the hair dryer and turned it on. The warm air pushed through the damp strands, warming her scalp. She closed her eyes, savoring the experience. When she opened them again, she flicked her gaze to the mirror and noticed a figure slip into her room. She jerked in surprise so hard she fell off the vanity stool and landed on the carpet with a startled yelp.

"Tash?" she heard Nathan call from the hallway, followed by footsteps hurrying toward her room. "Are you okay?"

She opened her mouth to scream for help, only to recognize her intruder a second later. There was no mistaking those bright golden eyes. A knock came at her door. She waved frantically for her visitor to disappear back into the shadows of the balcony right about the same time Nathan popped his head into her room.

"What are you doing on the floor?" her twin asked.

Realizing her bathrobe had ridden up during her less-than-graceful tumble, Natasha picked herself up and smoothed everything out, including her hair. Only one side was dry. The other side still hung in damp, limp strands over her shoulder. She flicked her gaze toward the balcony. The door was closed. She made a mental note to add a lock on the damn thing.

"I . . . um . . ." She returned her gaze to Nathan, who looked at her quizzically. "What are you still doing here? Shouldn't you be with Preston by now?"

She hoped to God the mention of his boyfriend was more

than enough to get Nathan off the fact that the curtains were open. She hated to have to explain to him what Jackson was doing on her balcony should her brother glance that way. Unless the jerk decided to leave the same way he came.

She shoved the thought away. Jackson coming to see her meant he wanted something. What that something was she had no idea, but seeing him again so soon did strange things to her heart—mainly making it pitter-patter annoyingly.

"Are you sure you're okay?" Nathan came forward and searched her face, concern on his own.

"I'm fine." Natasha slapped a hand in the air at him. "I just sat down wrong and slipped. I must be more tired than I thought."

He sighed. "Well, get some rest. You wouldn't want to be looking all red-eyed and puffy tomorrow."

"Y-yeah." Natasha laughed nervously.

Her brother's lips quirked. "By the way, I've made up my mind."

"Oh?" Another nervous laugh. Then she twirled a strand of hair. "About what?"

"Since Jackson is in town, I've decided to cancel my flight back to Colorado."

"You're staying in DoCo?" Elation and uncertainty warred for a place in her chest. "I totally welcome the emotional support, but you don't have to babysit me. I promise this won't be a repeat of last year. Jackson coming home doesn't change anything. I'm over him."

Yet the last part sounded hollow to her ears. The pain was still clearly there, as evidenced by the bathroom breakdown. But crying did her good. It centered her. Helped her focus.

"I know." Nathan pulled her into his arms and gave her a tight hug. "But indulge me and my peace of mind. As long as that shitface is anywhere near you, I'd like to run interference."

"Shitface?" Natasha leaned back, eyebrow raised.

Nathan shrugged. "I can curse too, you know."

"Don't. It's scaring the crap out of me."

He rolled his eyes. "Are you sure you're fine?"

"I am." She turned him around and placed both hands on his back, nudging him toward the door. "Now go. If you're staying, I'm sure you'll want to spend all the time you have left with Preston before he leaves."

Nathan gave her a suspicious glance over his shoulder before he left her room. She shut the door behind him, spinning around and leaning against it. Holding her breath, she counted to ten before exhaling.

"Is he gone?" came a whisper from the balcony.

Jerking in surprise again, Natasha pulled her robe tighter around her before making her way to the balcony. After taking a steadying deep breath, she peered through the glass pane. There, standing next to the door, was the reason for her heartbreak. Her earlier anger reared its ugly head.

"What are you doing here?" she hissed.

"Can I come in?" he asked back.

"No."

"Tash."

"No!" She covered her mouth when the word came out a little too loudly.

Nathan's room wasn't too far away, and she had no idea if he was still nearby. In fact, if her brother stepped out onto his own balcony, Jackson might as well jump, because there was no stopping Nathan from coming after him. Natasha flung open one of the doors, grabbed the front of Jackson's jacket, and yanked him in.

"Hey, I'm really sorry about the dress," he said.

"There's no saving a Valentino. It's ruined."

"Then I'll buy you another one."

Her lungs stopped working properly. The longer she stood in his presence, the more he affected her. Whether it was positive or negative, she couldn't tell. She squared her shoulders and lifted her chin. She let her anger push away whatever residual feelings she might have for Jackson. Let him stay in town all he wanted, she didn't care.

"Jax!" she barked.

"I wanted to give you these." He handed her the bouquet in his hands.

"Where did you get those?" She eyed the familiar-looking blooms, not taking them.

"At the party. I really needed to see you."

Natasha didn't know if she should be pissed or amused. On the one hand, Jackson bringing flowers to a fight was so like him. On the other hand, the jerk didn't even know that he was holding flowers she had given Adeline earlier. She went with pissed.

She scowled at him. "You came all this way to do what?"

"I was thinking maybe we can talk?"

"You want to talk?" Her voice rose with each word she spoke. "Well, that's not going to happen. Ever."

Like what she did to Nathan, she turned Jackson around and placed her hands on his back. But instead of gentle nudges, she shoved him hard until he was out on the balcony again.

"What are you doing?" Jackson asked in a panic.

"I'm kicking you out."

"Five minutes. Just give me five minutes. Two!"

She pointed out into the night. "You climbed up here on your own, so you can climb back down on your own. I'll give you extra points if you jump."

"Tash, please forgive me. I was wrong. About everything."

"You have some nerve asking me to do that."

"Let me make it up to you. I'll do anything. Anything."

"Like hell you will. Time is going to have to stop, gravity will have to fail, and the stars will have to come down before I ever consider forgiving a jerk like you." She slammed the balcony doors in his face. "And, by the way, your hair looks stupid!"

Jackson winced. The sound of Natasha closing the curtains on him seemed so loud. The hairs at the back of his neck prickled. He turned his head to face the balcony farther down the back wall, where a fuming Nathan stood with his arms crossed. Jackson raised one of his hands in surrender, the other still holding on to the bouquet.

"I'm going," he said.

"What kind of an idiot regifts flowers?" Nathan replied in disgust.

"What?"

Natasha's twin pointed at the bouquet. "Natasha gave those to Adeline at the party."

Jackson dropped his arms and stared at the bouquet. "Shit."

Six

TWELVE HOURS AND a mental note to buy his own goddamn flowers later, Jackson took a cab to the storage facility by the airport. He picked up his motorcycle and rode back toward town. Along the way he stopped at the WELCOME TO DODGE COVE sign, where he stood, staring at the road that led to the place he had been determined never to see again.

When he'd left, he thought it was for good. He was following his dream. Making a name for himself. But a year later, there he was, a few steps shy of the wasteland. Or promised land, depending on his state of mind.

"Welcome home," he mumbled.

The aviators he wore colored everything a dim blue. Just like his mood. The fingers on his hips tapped a restless beat. Sitting on his ass did him no good. If coming home gave him the chance to rediscover his music and convince the girl he loved not to hate him, then he was all for it.

So he strode back to his bike, swung a leg over the seat, pulled his helmet on, and kick-started the engine. The roaring rumble soothed his drumming heartbeat. Lifting his feet off the ground, he crossed the town line.

The bittersweet side of riding through town came in the form of memories at every corner. The record store he'd frequented still stood, its neon sign flickering. Diners he'd eaten at on the way to gigs out of town. The closest club was an hour away. And spots where he'd discovered how to love and be loved. Places where friendships were tested.

Ghosts of his past haunted him at forty miles an hour. In his periphery, it always seemed like he saw a familiar face or a cascade of sable hair. At a stoplight, his heart sputtered when he spotted a girl in a powder-blue dress, only to realize it wasn't *her*. Then his gaze landed on a familiar two-story brick building. The old music store where he'd learned to play the guitar had closed down. A FOR SALE sign hung on the door.

As he rode away, he mourned the store's closing. It seemed not everything was the same. His initial encounters with Natasha and his friends had definitely put the effects of his leaving into perspective. First day back was officially a disaster.

Soon he was back at the huge wrought-iron gates of Mallory Manor. Two *M*s were incorporated into the metalwork design. The gravel path crunched beneath the wheels of his bike. Fairy lights dangled from fully grown sycamore trees. There were fifty of them in all—spaced evenly along each side of the driveway.

The night before, he'd been so distracted about being home that he hadn't taken the time to notice the sprawling three-story mansion. Its gray stone and arched windows had intimidated him as a kid. Everything looked so big. Upon his return, the house was just a house.

Jackson maneuvered the bike into the garage, passing the black SUV his father used for official business, his mother's white Mercedes, his father's white Mercedes—matching his mother's, only in a different class—and his brother's black Audi. It seemed everyone was home.

Taking a deep breath, he removed his helmet and hung it on the hook specially bolted into the wall for it. Then he swung his leg over the bike and left the garage.

On tired legs, he approached what had once been his home. The massive crystal chandelier hanging above the marble foyer he entered. The area rug that was usually spread out at the center of the floor had been removed, along with the round table that always featured a flower arrangement of some kind. It made sense, since the day before an army of servers and staff had come in and out of the house, tracking in dirt with them.

"Jackie?"

Jackson's heart leapt into his throat and beat there for several seconds before it plummeted to the deepest reaches of his stomach. Slowly, he turned to face his mother. The pearls around her neck were the size of a baby's fist.

He ran his fingers through his hair. "Hey, Mom."

The look in her eyes was a mixture of happiness and concern. Her heels clicked on the marble floor when she finally approached and placed her hands on either side of his face. Her palms were as soft and smooth as he remembered. He leaned into the touch.

"You look tired," she said with motherly concern. "And

you've lost weight. Are you okay? Do you need to see a doctor?"

He shook his head to dispel the building panic in her expression. How the gentle woman before him worked as his father's campaign manager, Jackson had never managed to figure out.

"I'm fine," he said, squeezing her hand in both of his. "I'm sorry about how awkward everything got yesterday."

"You're staying?"

He hated the hurt in her voice. Besides Natasha, his mother might have been the one most devastated by him leaving. She had always been supportive. Always willing to give Jackson what he wanted.

"Yes," he said.

"Just make sure to let me know when you're leaving again, okay?"

When. It seemed like she didn't believe him. That in itself was a blow. Maybe, instead of insisting, he would just prove to her that he was in town to stay.

"I'm sorry I hurt you, Mom. I'm sorry I didn't say good-bye."

"Oh, Jackie." She pulled him into her arms.

Even if he towered over her by several inches, he went willingly. It was like he was five again. "If you'll have me, I'd like to stay."

"This is your home. You will always have a place here."

He held on for a little while longer, breathing in her fresh lily scent, before he stepped back. "Preston told me about the engagement party."

His mother put on her business face. "We sent you an invitation."

"Never got it. Would have RSVP'd if I had."

"That's odd. It says on the delivery sheet that your manager accepted it."

Hutch got the invite and didn't tell him? But why?

"I'm sorry I didn't get the invitation," he said, true remorse in his tone.

"That doesn't matter now." His mother shook her head.

He grinned at her, then gave her a kiss on the cheek. Then he turned and climbed up the stairs.

"Jackie."

He paused about halfway up and glanced over his shoulder. From the way she smiled up at him, he swore there were tears in her eyes.

"It's good to have you home," she said.

"It's good to be back." And he wasn't lying.

When he reached the top of the stairs, he veered right to the east wing. On the way to his room, his phone vibrated in his pocket. He pulled it out and stared at the screen. Brow furrowed, his thumb hovered over the green circle. A second later, he accepted the call.

"Hutch," he said.

"Where the hell are you?" his manager screamed.

Jackson placed his hand on his hip, widening his stance and looking up at the ceiling. "I'm back in Dodge Cove."

"What the fuck are you doing there?"

"Why didn't you tell me my brother was having an engagement party? My mother says you received the invitation."

"Jax, you were working." His manager's voice moved from anger to agitation. "The last thing I thought you needed was a distraction."

Lips in a tight line, Jackson said, "A distraction? Hutch, my brother's engagement is not a *distraction*." He rubbed his forehead. "You know what . . . clear my schedule for the rest of the year. I need a break."

"You can't do—"

Jackson ended the call before his manager finished the sentence. With his head still tipped toward the ceiling, he closed his eyes and breathed. When he bowed his head and opened his eyes, his shoulders slumped. He scratched the corner of his phone against the shaved side of his head. The rasp the device made against his short hair lifted some of the weight off his chest.

There were so many things he needed to do, and getting back to work wasn't one of them. He headed straight to his room and locked himself in.

Seven

NATASHA SPENT THE rest of the weekend after the engagement party in bed, watching reality TV and digging into several pints of Ben & Jerry's. She had nothing better to do. There were only so many trips to the salon she could do. And shopping didn't hold as much fun when it was all she did. Of course, there were a myriad of events happening in town at any given moment, but what was the point of attending? Same people. Same questions. Same lies for answers.

Come Monday, she had been prepared to spend the rest of the week in her room. The truth was: she wasn't really fine. More like lost. She had no idea what she was going to do after her gap year. And Jackson "The Abandoner" Mallory was back in town. That was her life in a nutshell, and it was increasingly looking like a pathetic existence.

"Are you seriously going to spend the entire day in bed?" asked her mother, who strode into the room and yanked the curtains open, letting in early afternoon light.

Natasha pointed at the TV with her spoon. "Tim is about to give this designer a make-it-work moment."

"I heard Jackson was back in town," her mother added nonchalantly, like she was commenting on the weather.

"Yeah, well, I'm staying in bed until he leaves."

Her mom clucked her tongue. "If you do that, then you might as well admit that he won. I thought I raised you to be a stronger woman than someone who wallows in bed because her ex decided to make an appearance."

"It's not like I have anything on my schedule worth doing."

"Let me see . . ." Her mother counted off with her fingers. "There are your debutante duties. I'm sure Adeline can always use your help with something."

Natasha imitated the sound of a buzzer on a game show going off. The she spooned another mouthful of pralines and cream into her mouth.

"There's the Dodge Cove Preservation Society dinner tonight."

Again the buzzer went off. Natasha added a pout for effect.

Her mother sighed. "Then you might as well make yourself useful and bring Mrs. Winchester her groceries for the week. You can at least do that, can't you? I would do it, but I have a Matrons meeting."

Natasha sucked on her spoon before she answered, "How long will you bug me about this if I don't get up?"

The mischief in her mother's eyes was so similar to Nathan's. Seriously, it was like looking in a mirror to find an older, blond version of herself. Natasha rolled her eyes in dramatic fashion.

"If I do this," she said, because two could play this game, "you don't get to bug me about anything for the rest of the week."

Yet even with the condition out there in the open, it still seemed like her mother won when she said, "Done!"

Sighing heavily, Natasha leaned to the side and deposited the half-eaten pint on the nightstand. Then she pushed aside the covers and marched toward the bathroom.

"The groceries are in the kitchen," her mother called after her in triumph.

Half an hour later, Natasha left the Tesla just outside the ivy-covered walls of Winchester Place. It seemed rude to just drive up to the house since she wasn't as close to the Winchesters as her parents were. The driveway was a short walk anyway. She balanced one grocery bag on each arm and bumped the car door closed with her hip.

At least the gate was left open. Not that she thought it was for her arrival. It seemed the gate hadn't been closed for some time. It creaked when she nudged it. Remembering the gravel along the pathway, she'd opted for sturdy, lace-up espadrilles in lieu of the pumps she usually paired with her pale-blue eyelet dress with cap sleeves. The hem kissed her knees when she moved.

At the door, the owl knocker stared at her. She lowered the groceries on either side of her, smoothed the front of her dress, and swung the braid of her hair over one shoulder. Then she reached for the brass ring in the owl's beak, knocked three times, and waited.

When a minute passed without a response, she checked for

a doorbell and found none. She stepped back from the front door and surveyed her surroundings. Despite the glowing afternoon sun, a certain gloom loomed over the property. She wanted to get the task over with and return to binge-watching her overflowing DVR.

"Hello," she called. "Anyone home?"

Natasha tried the knocker again. The door opened an inch. She smiled, expecting the butler's face. When empty air greeted her, she frowned and craned her neck.

"Hello?" she asked, sounding unsure of herself.

"Down here."

Startled, Natasha dropped her gaze to meet a boy about four feet tall wearing thick black-rimmed glasses. He had a pale face and straight brown hair.

"Hi," Natasha said. She bent down so they were at eye level, and she noticed that the boy had the clearest gray eyes she had ever seen. "You must be Albert. I'm Natasha Parker. My mom sent me over with these groceries. Is your mom around?"

"Mom's in the glass room."

"Glass room?"

Albert opened the door farther and stepped aside. He wore a white button-down with tan slacks. But the striking thing was the yellow-and-red scarf around his neck.

"Yeah," he said. "The one with glass walls with plants in it."

"Oh, you mean the solarium."

He shrugged. "Want me to show you the way?"

"That would be great. Thanks," she said, picking up the groceries and balancing one bag in each arm.

She remembered how Nate, Caleb, and Preston used to be when they were Albert's age. They were full of energy.

Rambunctious. Out of control, most of the time. Like typical ten-year-olds. Albert seemed the opposite of that as he led the way farther into the house after closing the door.

Despite the windows, the light didn't seem to reach all the way inside. As they passed the living room and the dining room, Natasha noted the bare walls. Only the faint outline of the frames remained.

"Where are the paintings?" she asked, mostly to herself. She didn't think she had spoken loud enough until Albert replied.

"In the attic. Mom put them all up there."

"Why?"

He shrugged, his little shoulders going up an inch.

When they finally reached the solarium, the sound of quiet sobbing reached Natasha's ears. She froze. Albert did too.

"She's been like that since I came home from school today," he whispered.

Natasha recognized the pain without having to see into the solarium. She tightened her grip on the grocery bags and squared her shoulders. Albert didn't need to witness his mother in such a vulnerable state.

"Albert, why don't you take me to the kitchen instead?" Natasha asked in a gentle tone. "We can put away these groceries."

Without another word, Albert turned around and walked past her. Natasha quickly followed after him. The kitchen was just nearby. He entered first.

Natasha stopped at the threshold. The sink was filled with unwashed dishes. Pizza boxes and Chinese takeout containers littered the center island, along with what seemed like dozens of untouched casseroles.

"Wow," she said under her breath. "Where's that smell coming from?"

"Mom fired Foster and the staff a week ago," Albert said simply, as if it explained the unbelievable mess.

Natasha thought back to a time when in a fit of grief Caleb's father had done the same thing. "Oh. That's too bad."

"Yeah."

"All right." She straightened to her full height. "Why don't you and me roll up our sleeves and surprise your mom by cleaning this place up?"

"Do I have to?"

"I won't take no for an answer." Natasha used a sterner tone. "Grab a trash bag and dump every empty container of food inside while I get started on the dishes."

Albert did as he was told. Natasha stifled a smile. He was a good kid. It must have been tough seeing his mom cry and even tougher still to be mourning his dad too. His helplessness called to her; she recognized it as the same feeling she'd gone through a year ago. She left the groceries by the door and headed straight for the sink. At least cleaning the kitchen would mean one less thing Mrs. Winchester had to worry about.

She found yellow gloves under the sink, put them on, and got to work. A part of her was glad her mother had sent her the Winchesters' way. She welcomed anything that kept her mind off thinking about Jackson. *Project Runway* could wait.

When Albert came back inside after throwing out the two trash bags he'd filled, he joined Natasha at the sink and began loading the dishwasher.

"Thanks," she said as she rinsed another plate.

Albert merely shrugged and kept working.

Wanting to relieve some of the tension, Natasha asked, "So how's school?"

Except for the scarf, Albert's uniform was from her old private school. It must have been tough for him to be back in a classroom when it had been only a few weeks since the funeral. But then again, maybe school was a refuge for Albert away from the gloom of their home.

"Entrepreneurship Day is coming up," he grumbled, placing the plate she handed him into the rack along with the others he'd already loaded into the dishwasher.

"Oh!" Natasha brightened. "I remember those. What will you be selling?"

Another shrug.

Natasha's heart dropped, but she continued. "Our Entrepreneurship Day fell during the week of Valentine's Day, so we decided to sell Valentine's cards with the option of having them hand-delivered to the recipients. We sold them for five bucks apiece."

"That's nice," he said, no enthusiasm in his voice whatsoever.

"There must be something you're interested in."

No response. Albert was so small for his age that the plate in his hands seemed so big. Her heart squeezed. She wanted to bundle him up and tell him everything was going to be okay. But he might not take the concern well from a relative stranger. Instead she committed herself to helping him.

"What's with the scarf?" she asked, steering the subject to something he might be interested in.

After a beat, he said, "It's Gryffindor House."

"I have to confess that I'm not much of a Harry Potter fan," she said with a smile.

Albert's eyes widened, as if she just confessed to hating puppies. "You don't like Harry Potter?"

"I never got into the books. But my boy—" Natasha pressed her lips together, then started again. "But my *ex*-boyfriend is a big fan. He actually lined up at midnight for the last book."

"My dad bought me the last book." Albert's face fell.

"Oh, well . . ." She floundered at first. Then the idea struck her. "Why not a lemonade stand?"

He grimaced.

"Hear me out," she insisted. "Since you like Harry Potter, we can call it wizardade or something. My mom has this great lemonade recipe we can use. She adds club soda to give it a fizzy kick. And we can also sell cookies and cupcakes and name them after characters in the books."

The more she spoke, the less sad Albert seemed, until he finally listened to her intently. Pretty soon, he was making suggestions like the stand could be in Gryffindor colors and he could dress up as Harry Potter. All of which Natasha said yes to, because it was his project. They made plans to meet up the next day and get started on making the booth, since Entrepreneurship Day was at the end of the week.

It didn't slip Natasha's mind that creating the booth would be so much easier with Jackson's help: He was the Harry Potter expert. But like hell was she going to ask him. Just thinking of him made her so mad. She'd rather read all seven books in one night than ask him for help!

Eight

JACKSON RODE AROUND Dodge Cove to clear his head Monday evening, searching for ideas. He rode without any real destination. The Harley-Davidson Daytona had served him well on so many midnight rides. Only about a thousand of them were ever made. The bike was distinctive for its front wheel sticking out, curved handlebar, and yellow chrome finish. When the rest of the guys got cars, he got a badass bike. He'd found it at a junkyard for next to nothing and spent a summer putting it back together.

His home might have stayed the same, but everything else in his life seemed different. Especially Natasha. She looked good. Damn good. Maybe even better. A year without him had changed her, and he didn't know how he felt about it. All he really knew was that he needed her back in his life. How he'd lasted a year without her was impossible to make sense of. The last six months had certainly been hell.

Confused and more than a little lost, Jackson rode to the Grant Estate at the crack of dawn. Leaving the bike on the gravel path, he snuck into the detached building of the indoor pool like a thief in the night. Splashing drew him to the water.

Since Preston and Nathan had decided to live together in Colorado, Jackson envied them. Their love story had started right around the same time his and Natasha's did. They might not have figured out their feelings for each other as fast, but Jackson knew Preston felt for Nathan the same way he felt for Natasha. How Jackson had ever let go of that kind of love was completely insane.

Stepping to the pool's edge, Jackson waited until its occupant reached him.

"Jesus!" Preston yelled, slapping the water in surprise. He yanked off his goggles and cap and glared up at Jackson. "Fuck you for scaring the shit out of me."

Jackson laughed. "Hello to you too."

Preston gripped the edge of the pool with both hands and hauled himself out. Jackson stepped back and grabbed a towel from a stack beside one of the lounge chairs. Grinning, he tossed the towel over to Preston. The swimmer caught it without flinching. Then Jackson stretched out onto one of the chaises, cradling his head in his arms.

"You need to teach your boyfriend to curse better," Jackson said. "He called me a shitface when he and Tash were talking. Not that I didn't deserve it."

"You have to admit, you are kind of a shitface."

"I don't remember you being this cranky after a swim. Does this have to do with the fact that Nate is staying in DoCo?"

Preston wiped the towel down his face and said, "How did you know about that?"

"The balcony doors aren't that thick. I'm sorry, man."

"He thinks you're here to hurt Tash again." Preston took a seat on the lounge chair to Jackson's right. He slung the towel over his shoulders and leaned forward until his forearms rested on his knees. "I keep telling him that you want her back, but he doesn't believe me. Even chewed my ear off because I'm still in contact with you."

"Thanks for sticking by me," Jackson said. He closed his eyes for a second and sighed. When he opened them again, he stared at the purplish-pink sky over the glass ceiling. "To be honest, if you hadn't knocked some sense into me in those texts, I don't know what I would have done. I left because I thought I was doing the right thing. Going on tour? That was the dream, man. But seeing Tash in Amsterdam was a reality check. No matter how many gigs I do, none of it makes sense without her."

The swimmer sighed, shaking his head. "Honestly, I didn't think you would listen to me, but I'm glad you did. I think she needs you just as much as you need her."

Rubbing his face with both hands, Jackson asked, "How can you tell? Because from where I'm standing, all I can see is I hurt her and she hates me."

Preston punched him playfully on the arm. "That doesn't mean you should give up, right? I grew up watching you two. If there are people who fit together best—besides me and Nate—it's you and Tash. I'm pretty sure that behind all that hate and hurt, she's just as lost as you are."

"Caleb told me that Tash was a total mess after I left."

"It was bad. She's come a really long way since then."

A corner of Jackson's lips tugged up. "Yeah. Not being with her for a year was hard enough. I didn't realize being in the same room with her without being able to hold and kiss her would be worse."

Preston's eyebrows pushed together. "What do you expect? Of course there's some blowback. Just hang in there."

"Things have to change, man." Jackson meant every word. "*I* have to change or I'm looking at a dead end."

"Care to elaborate?"

Jackson sat up. "When I left, I thought I was living the life. You know? Then I realized all that means crap without my friends. Without . . ."

Preston studied him intently. "So what do you plan to do about it?"

Swinging his legs over the side, Jackson faced his friend and said, "She actually told me that I will have to stop time, defy gravity, and bring down the stars before she will consider forgiving me."

A low whistle followed Jackson's words.

"Yeah."

"That's tough, bro."

Jackson rubbed his jaw. "Tell me about it. I just wish there was something more I could do, you know? She doesn't want to talk to me, so I'm going to have to show her that I'm serious about getting her back. It has to be something big. Flowers and chocolate just won't cut it."

Preston frowned. "I can't help you there. I'm not much of a romantic. Nathan is the fan of grand gestures."

"Don't say that." Jackson smacked him on the arm

good-naturedly. "What about that time you confessed your feelings for him?"

"That wasn't a grand gesture. It was telling him the truth. Plus, I had some help." Then Preston's eyes grew wide. "But you already have all the help you need."

"What do you mean?" But as soon as the question left Jackson's mouth, Preston's words clicked in his head. "Stopping time. Defying gravity. Bringing down the stars."

"Exactly!" Preston frowned. "But it's all impossible."

"No . . ." Jackson cracked his knuckles. "No, it's not. I just have to really think about it. Can you imagine? If I pull all this off, maybe she'll actually forgive me." He jumped to his feet and started walking toward the door. "This is going to be awesome!"

"What are you going to do?" Preston asked.

"Three grand gestures to win back the girl I love."

Nine

NATASHA GASPED AWAKE. She sat up with eyes squinted, looking around her room. A Post-it stuck to her cheek. In the background, her laptop was still playing the audiobook version of *Harry Potter and the Goblet of Fire*. On her bed were dozens of other Post-its and other notes. She'd spent all night doing her research and fell down the rabbit hole of a website called Harry Potter Wiki. Who knew such a thing existed?

Her mind buzzed with a million pieces of information. She'd thought if she crammed all night she'd be ready to help Albert with his lemonade stand. Unfortunately, nothing seemed to make sense to her. All the notes. What the narrator was saying about Harry fighting a dragon. She rubbed her face and pulled off the Post-it on her cheek right about the same time her gaze landed on her digital clock. The screen was blank. Why was the screen blank?

As she tried to remember when she had unplugged her clock, her hands felt around for her phone. Once her fingers made contact, she brought the device to her face and squinted at the numbers. Even if her brain was still half-asleep, she could make out the numbers one and thirty.

"Holy crap!"

Fully awake, she scrambled out of bed and tripped on her sheets. Pain exploded in her knees. She winced. But the panic of having to meet Albert in a couple of hours shot her with enough adrenaline to propel her into the bathroom. She still had to buy the art supplies, and Didi was already waiting for her at the art store.

After splashing some water on her face, she turned in a tight circle inside her closet. No time to plan a proper outfit, so she picked out a pair of skinny jeans, a graphic tee, and a pair of sneakers.

She quickly gathered all her hair into a ponytail. No time for makeup either. Lip gloss and a smile would have to do. She smacked her lips together, grabbed her bag, and rushed out of her room at the same time Nathan entered the hallway. Since he still seemed out of it, Natasha turned on her heel slowly and made a run for it.

"Hey!" He pointed at her, wide-eyed. She winced and stopped at the end of the hall. "Don't think you can escape me, young lady. We have a ton to talk about. Granted, this conversation is overdue, since I was with Preston all weekend until he left for Colorado yesterday."

"Nate, can this wait? I'm in a rush."

"I saw Jackson climbing down your trellis. So, what? You had a little midnight rendezvous?"

She turned around to face her brother. "Jackson was in my room, big deal. He used to do it all the time."

"Yeah, but it's the lying to me about it that I can't stand." Nathan stormed to her and grabbed ahold of her bag. "Were you planning on keeping it from me?"

Natasha gripped the strap with both hands and dug her heels in. "Of course not!"

Nathan pulled. "Who are you kidding?"

Using her hips to pivot, she yanked the bag out of his grasp. "Nate, I seriously don't want to get into this. If you saw him climbing down the trellis, then you know that I kicked him out. I don't want anything to do with him."

Worry filled his eyes. "Tash, I just don't want him to break your heart again. That's all."

"As if I'd let him get close to my heart." She resettled her bag straps on her shoulder.

"Just say the word. I know a good spot to hide a body."

"I love you, Nate." Natasha planted a kiss on his cheek. "I'm a big girl. I can take care of myself. Let me handle Jackson. Okay?"

"I'm saying yes." Nathan rested his hands on his hips. "But under protest. I'm keeping an eye on him."

"I wouldn't expect anything less." She smiled. "Now, I have to go. I'm already late."

She hurried down the stairs and headed straight for the kitchen.

"Hey, jelly bean!" her father greeted her from the breakfast nook, the paper in one hand and a mug of coffee in the other. "Good afternoon."

"Hey, Dad." She gave him a kiss on the cheek. "Did you just get back, or are you just about to leave?"

"Just making a few rounds at the hospital today. Nothing major. Then your mom and I are going on a date."

Her dad looked dashing in a navy-blue suit and a yellow tie. The color brightened the blue of his eyes. His dark brown hair, salted with white strands, only served to make him look more distinguished.

Natasha grabbed an apple from the bowl on the table and said, "You two have fun."

"Got any big plans today?"

"Building a lemonade stand," Natasha said as she left the kitchen.

Munching on the apple, she opened the front door and stepped out of the house. Then she froze at the landing by the front steps.

"Oh, give me a break!" She almost dropped the apple.

Parked on the driveway was Jackson, leaning against his motorcycle. He seemed chipper, smiling at her like a guy who'd gotten a full eight hours the night before. Because, unlike her, he'd read all the Harry Potter books. Not that he would know she spent all night learning everything there was to learn about the boy wizard. Seeing him when she was already late just annoyed her even more.

"Hi," Jackson said, flashing that sexy grin that never failed to make her knees quake.

Lifting her chin, Natasha jogged down to the driveway and veered right, toward her car.

"Where are you going?" Jackson pushed away from the bike and followed after her.

"I don't think that's any of your business," she said, unlocking her Tesla.

The lights flashed twice. A large hand on the door handle prevented her from wrapping her fingers around it.

"Jax." She looked up at him. "I'm really busy today, and I'm already late. Please move."

There was a moment of hesitation before he grabbed her bag, stuffed it into the backseat, and shut the door. Then a flash of determination crossed his expression. It made her nervous. He rounded the back of the SUV, opened the passenger door, and slid into the seat.

"What are you doing?" she asked after opening her own door.

Jackson buckled himself in. "You said you were late. Get in."

"Get out of the car, Jackson. I mean it."

"No."

"I seriously don't have time for this crap. Get out of the car or so help me—"

"You'll what?" he challenged, mischief transforming his face into that boy she'd grown up with. "You know I'll just follow you on my bike. This way we're saving the environment by carpooling." Before she could respond, he raised both his hands in surrender. "I promise I won't bug you. I'm just along for the ride."

"Ugh!" Natasha got into the car and slammed the door shut. She knew quite well the lengths Jackson went to when he was determined. If she showed him that he no longer mattered in her life, then maybe he might leave her alone. Unfortunately, the breath she took was filled with his clean boy scent, flooding her mind with images of lying in his arms during countless summer nights.

"This might be harder than I thought," she muttered under her breath.

"Huh?"

But from the glint in his eyes, it was obvious he'd heard her. In revenge, she handed him the half-eaten apple and cranked up the Taylor Swift. The pained expression on Jackson's face filled her with sick satisfaction as she slipped on her sunglasses and drove down the cherry-blossom-lined driveway.

Ten minutes later, Natasha eased the SUV into one of the last slots available in front of an art supply store. Jackson's molars hurt from all the heartbreak revenge songs, but he was all for listening to them if it meant being in the car with Natasha. Her hair smelled of strawberries. It gave him comfort that she hadn't changed her shampoo in the twelve months they had been apart.

Jackson had thought there was no way Natasha could ignore him for the *whole* car ride. But she surprised him. She even refused to dance along to her favorite Taylor Swift song. That was cold.

Resting his elbow against the door and resting his chin on his fist, he secretly watched her in his peripheral vision. The shirt she wore bared her arms, giving him a perfect view of the sprinkling of freckles on her shoulders that drove him crazy. His lips missed being on them, kissing each one. But Natasha wasn't in that head space anymore. Leaning over and planting kisses on her shoulder wasn't the turn-on it used to be for her. He knew it in his gut. In fact, giving in to the urge might just get him smacked in the face and send him back to square one with her.

He took her allowing him to ride along as a step forward. A vast improvement since the blunder of sneaking into her room. Of course, she had only driven off with him in the car because she was massively late. But still, it was progress.

All morning he'd thought about proving to her that he was serious. Nothing was going to stop him from getting her back. Like the air he breathed, he needed her.

The instant she cut the engine, Taylor Swift singing that they were "never ever, ever getting back together" stopped. Jackson barely stifled the sigh of relief that begged to break out of his lungs. Even he knew sending the wrong message was the worst move. So, instead he decided to state the obvious.

"Art store?"

Natasha turned her head to face him. Her lips were the pink he loved. The color emphasized the bow shape. And it might not be the manliest thought, but he secretly liked how when they kissed the color stained his lips. He wore it like a badge of honor. A sign to the world that the gorgeous girl with him was his and only his.

"All right, you're still not speaking to me. I get that. So I'll have to talk for the both of us."

She rolled her eyes, unbuckled her seat belt, and slipped out of the car. If there was a way to tell him he was an idiot, that was it, right there. But damn if she wasn't being cute when giving him the cold shoulder.

"Hey, wait up!" Jackson scrambled after her.

Ten

NATASHA SWORE JACKSON was doing it on purpose. She'd felt his eyes on her the entire time they were in the car. Ugh! He drove her nuts. Why couldn't he just leave her alone?

Everything seemed familiar and foreign all at once. In the car, it felt like sitting with a stranger and her best friend. Because when Jackson left, not only had she lost a boyfriend, she had lost one of the best people in her life. A guy who knew every part of her. Knew what she was thinking even before she verbalized it.

And just like that, she was back to hating him again. She held on to the emotion as she pushed into the store. It must get her through. The bell at the door jingled jauntily, announcing their arrival.

"You're late," Didi said from the counter.

"I picked up a hitchhiker along the way." Natasha pointed her thumb over her shoulder to indicate Jackson, who ambled in after her like a jungle cat. The way he moved was enough to make anyone swoon.

"We haven't formally met," Jackson said in that deep as molasses voice of his. He reached out across the counter. "Jackson Mallory, the current bane of everyone's existence."

"Under these circumstances, it's lukewarm to meet you," Didi replied, taking his hand for a firm shake. "I'm Diana, but they all call me Didi. You, on the other hand, may refer to me as your worst nightmare if you so much as step out of line and hurt Tash."

Immediately, he held up his hands and took a step back for good measure. "I'll keep that in mind."

Didi pursed her lips against the patented panty-melting Jackson grin. "Caleb's right, you're a smooth operator. Normally, this is the time when I'd offer to paint you, but I haven't made up my mind yet. You're handsome enough."

"Thanks?" Jackson glanced at Natasha for backup.

As if she would give him any. Instead she grabbed a basket from the counter. "Cardboard at the back?"

Didi nodded. "Paintbrushes are in aisle eight and paint supplies in nine. Holler if you're looking for anything specific."

"Thanks," Natasha said as she made her way down the aisle of scrapbooking supplies.

"What do we need?" Jackson asked, walking a step behind her.

The aisles weren't wide enough to fit two people shoulder to shoulder, which Natasha was secretly thankful for. Being in such close quarters was tough enough.

She paused at the brushes. Jackson grabbed the basket out of her hand.

"Hey!" She scowled at him.

He raised his free hand.

She wanted to roll her eyes again, but she was seriously pressed for time, and the stress of having him there was causing her muscles to knot. So she crossed her arms and pinned him with a pointed glare.

"What?"

"Permission to speak?" he asked.

She waved her hand for him to continue.

Jackson took a deep breath and said, "I'm not going anywhere. You know I'm not going anywhere."

She opened her mouth to speak, but he stopped her with a raised finger. Eyebrow arching, she shut her lips and waited.

"You're already late," he continued. "Won't this go faster if you just let me help?"

Her first instinct was to refuse. She was capable enough to do everything herself. But as much as she hated to admit it, he was right. Albert must already be expecting her over at the Winchester mansion. And the amount of cardboard she would need was more than she could carry all at once.

"Fine," she huffed out, then grabbed a couple of brushes from the plastic containers that divided them into different sizes and caught Jackson performing a celebratory fist pump. "You're such an idiot."

"Where next, boss?"

Turning her back on him, she moved to the aisle where they kept the paint. According to her research, or what was left of her discombobulated brain, Gryffindor colors were scarlet and gold. She picked up two small cans for each.

"Red and gold?" Jackson asked. "Is there a theme to this secret project?"

"It's not a secret," she said as she moved to the back, where the cardboard was kept. "It's a lemonade stand."

A pause on Jackson's part as they reached the cardboard. He rubbed his chin, studying the different sizes. Natasha began flipping through the stacks.

"What kind of charity is the Debutante Society working with now that you have to build a lemonade stand from scratch?"

The questions were getting on her nerves. She knew she shouldn't have budged an inch. Jackson was taking a mile.

Not really focusing on what she was doing, Natasha shifted to her toes and reached for the topmost board on a large stack. She teetered and lost her balance. Arms flailing, she yelped as she fell backward. A strong pair of arms wrapped around her almost immediately, gathering her against a solid chest. Heart hammering, she looked up at Jackson. His head was bent toward hers. Their lips were so tantalizingly close.

"You okay?" he asked, concern on his face.

His warmth surrounded her like a blanket during a particularly chilly night. Her mind went blank for a second before her thoughts and emotions revved up again.

"L-let go," she said, wriggling like a kitten trapped in yarn. He was too close. "Let me go."

Jackson complied, stepping away. His arms remained close just in case . . . what? She lost her balance again? Well, that wasn't going to happen.

By sheer force of will, she widened her stance and straightened her spine. Then she flipped her ponytail over her shoulder and said, "This isn't for the Debs. I'm helping out a friend for Entrepreneurship Day."

As if she hadn't just been in his arms, Jackson blinked twice. "Entrepreneurship Day? Isn't that in grade school?"

"It's for Mrs. Winchester's son, Albert. He wants to do a Harry Potter–themed lemonade stand."

Actually, it was Natasha who'd convinced him to do the stand, but same difference. She realized her mistake of spilling too much, because Jackson's eyes lit up at the mention of the two magic words.

"That explains the paint!" He became animated. "You have to let me help. Please. I've read all the books more than once and I still watch the movies at least once a year and"—he paused before delivering the death blow—"I know the Harry Potter calligraphy style."

If this was a video game, Natasha's character had just been KO'd by Jackson's character and the word *WINNER* flashed at the center of the screen. No matter how hard she'd studied Harry Potter lore the night before, there was no beating the fact that Jackson knew the calligraphy. Of course he did.

"No," she said.

"What?" All the humor in Jackson's face left.

Natasha turned around and hurried to the front of the store. It was too much. Just being around him was too much. She didn't even hear what Didi was saying as she ran outside. She got into her car and drove away.

Armed with art supplies she bought at an art store a town over, Natasha stood outside the front door of Winchester Place. Albert was right there the second she used the knocker, a look of anticipation on his boyish face.

"Hello, Albert," Natasha greeted him with a smile.

"What took you so long?" he replied, a mix of worry and excitement in his tone.

Natasha didn't lose her smile for a second. "I'm already here, that's what matters. Let's get started on that stand."

Albert babbled on about how he wanted the stand. How the sign should look. He explained the meaning of scarlet and gold and how Gryffindor House stood for bravery, daring, nerve, and chivalry. And something called a sorting hat sorted Albert into Gryffindor.

"I have both colors right here," Natasha said, indicating the bag with the cans of paint, and Albert whooped for joy.

Since the other store she'd gone to was out of gold paint, Natasha suggested they use yellow. It was the closest to gold she could find. Albert sulked about it for about ten minutes but eventually gave in to the fact that Natasha had tried her best.

They worked on the lawn. Based on plans she downloaded off the Internet, Natasha cut out the appropriate pieces that made up all three sides and the roof of the stand. They laid out each piece on the grass. Albert was in charge of painting the larger pieces, while Natasha focused on the lettering for the sign.

She tilted her head, the tip of her tongue sticking out of the corner of her mouth. Her brow furrowed. Then she frowned.

Natasha was good at a lot of things, but lettering wasn't one of them. The word *LEMONADE* was crooked. The *O* blended into the *N*. The *T* and the *A* ran together, so the sign read LEMONADE SAND.

In paint-splattered overalls Didi would be proud of, Albert approached. "That's the sign?"

"Nope!" Natasha shoved the thick cardboard away and pulled out another piece. She had cut out several in anticipation of mistakes. "I'll keep trying until I get this just right. How are the sides coming along?"

"Painting stripes is easy," Albert said, sounding like someone older than his years. Like someone capable of doing anything.

Natasha glanced over to his side of the lawn, and indeed the red stripes along the sides and front of the stand were as straight as if they'd been drawn in using a ruler. He'd been about to start on the yellow when he came to check on the sign. Renewed determination filled her.

"Great job," she said, a little jealous. "Keep going. When they dry, we can glue the sides and front together."

"Are you sure you're okay with the sign?" Albert eyed her skeptically.

"I'm fine." Her smile wobbled, so she pressed her lips together. "More than fine. I'll make this sign perfect for you."

"You know you can't draw letters to save your life, right?" someone said from behind her.

The second she recognized the voice, Natasha closed her eyes and cursed under her breath. The guy was relentless. She wasn't even sure how he got there. Then she said, "What are you doing here?"

"Who's he?" Albert said, pushing his glasses up with the back of his hand, leaving a streak of paint along the bridge of his nose.

"Hey," Jackson said. "I'm—"

"Remember what your mother told you," Natasha warned, finally looking over her shoulder at Jackson. Her heart did a familiar flutter at the sight of him. She squashed the feeling like a bug. "Don't talk to strangers."

"She's right." Jackson's words came with a charming grin. "Talking to strangers is bad. For all you know I'm someone who has candy so I can kidnap you."

"Do you have candy?" Albert asked matter-of-factly.

Jackson made a show of patting his pockets. "Not at the moment, no."

Albert considered. "Are you going to kidnap me or Tash?"

"You, no. Tash, that's a different story."

"What's that mean?" Albert looked to Natasha, whose face felt hotter than a sidewalk on a summer day.

"You see," Jackson interjected before Natasha found the words to speak, "Tash and I are old, old friends. We met when we were way younger than you. Unfortunately, I did something bad and she got mad at me."

"Something bad?"

Natasha gave Jackson a warning glare, which he proceeded to ignore when he nodded and said, "Yeah. Sometimes people make mistakes. Hurting the ones they love."

Albert's face fell. "Like the time Dad and Mom had an argument because Dad didn't buy milk when Mom asked him to."

Jackson's smile twitched. "Something *like* that. I didn't buy the milk, so now I'm doing everything I can to make things right."

Albert nodded once, as if Jackson's words were the right thing to say. Natasha watched in annoyed awe. Jackson had always been a smooth operator. Kids under twelve never stood a chance against him.

"More like went out to buy milk and never returned," she muttered. From the glint in Jackson's eyes, he'd heard her. She sighed. "Albert, remember the friend I told you about who likes Harry Potter as much as you do? Well, meet Jackson. Jackson, meet Albert."

"What house are you?" Albert asked immediately, like it was some rite of passage.

"The house of daring, nerve, and chivalry," Jackson said with great reverence.

If Albert's gaze grew any wider, Natasha feared his eyes might fall out of their sockets. As much as she hated Jackson at the moment, she couldn't deny that he and Albert connected on a level she couldn't reach on her own. Damn Jackson for being adorable when he wanted to be.

"Gryffindor," Albert whispered in awe.

"Nice to meet you, Albert." Jackson reached out and they shook hands. "Wow! That's a great grip you've got there."

"Yeah?" Albert looked up at him, completely charmed.

"I like a man who knows how to shake hands." Jackson knelt so they were at eye level.

"My dad said a man should always have a firm handshake. It tells people you mean business." Albert's ears turned pink.

"My dad says the same thing." Jackson let go of Albert's

hand and reached for something in the bag he had been carrying. "I think someone needs more paint?" Albert jumped in place the instant Jackson produced two cans of gold paint from the bag and a couple of extra brushes. "Can't have Gryffindor colors without gold paint."

"Awesome!" Albert took the paint. "Thank you!"

Jackson sat on his haunches beside Natasha before he said to Albert, "Why don't you get started on the gold stripes? I'll take over with the lettering before Tash murders another 'Lemonade Sand' sign."

The boys shared a knowing grin before Albert left to get started on his task. Natasha stared the entire time, jaw dropped. Then she nudged Jackson on the shoulder.

"You stalker," she said, low enough for Albert not to hear.

"Move over." He reached for another blank board.

She eased out of the way just as he pulled out a pencil from the bag and on all fours began drawing letters in smooth, confident strokes.

"I thought leaving you at the store was answer enough to your offer to help," Natasha said, lifting her chin, unwilling to give in.

"Good thing I'm a rebel." He winked at her. "If I remember correctly, you used to love my rebellious side."

She smacked him on the shoulder. "Don't be a jerk."

"Hey!" He paused, pencil a few inches from the board. "You're going to make me mess up."

"What? You're using pencil. Don't you have an eraser in that bag of wonders of yours?"

Despite being annoyed that Jackson had followed her to the

Winchesters, the fact that he'd brought the paint they needed that she had left along with the first batch of supplies with him was indicative of how reliable he could be sometimes. *Sometimes*, she reminded herself. It was for Albert's sake that she didn't ask Jackson to leave. He was handy with a paintbrush, and he had said he knew the Harry Potter lettering.

With concentration all over his handsome face, he asked, "Hey, are you free this Friday?"

The question took her aback. She was about to ask him what he had in mind. It had always been her automatic response to the question of weekend plans. But she bit her tongue in time.

"Of course I'm not free," she said. "I have to help Albert with the lemonade stand for Entrepreneurship Day."

"Good. Because I need to show you something on Sunday."

She opened her mouth, only to realize that he had her there. The grin on his lips said so.

"I have plans on Sunday too, you know," she insisted, playing it cool.

"Town square. Meet me at the gazebo five minutes to noon."

"Why would I do that?"

He paused his work to look her in the eye when he said, "There's something I want to show you."

"Wha—"

"Is that my sign?" Albert asked, hopping from foot to foot in excitement.

"Do you like it?" Jackson asked back, indicating the lettering with a wave of the hand holding the pencil.

The sign featured block Gothic letters with swishes as accents over the lowercase letters. In between the words *lemonade* and *stand* was a shield that featured a lion standing on its hind legs.

"I used the calligraphy style on the covers and included the Gryffindor crest in the middle, since you like them so much," Jackson said, smiling.

"It's so cool!" Albert beamed.

"Wait until I'm done," Jackson said. "Since the stand is already in crimson and gold, why don't we paint the letters in black so they stand out more? Then I'll paint the crest in crimson and gold too."

"Thank you, thank you, thank you!"

Natasha pushed to her feet, a floaty feeling emanating from the center of her chest. "Let's leave him to it, then." She placed a hand on Albert's shoulder as he bounced in place. "I'll help you with the stand."

Without another word, Albert ran back to his painting. There was a giddiness surrounding the boy that hadn't been there when she'd first delivered groceries to the mansion. And the person responsible for it was already hard at work again.

"Thank you," she said grudgingly. She wasn't a monster. She gave credit where credit was due. Even if it was due to Jackson.

"Does this mean I'm forgiven?" he joked.

"Not by a long shot."

Natasha turned on her heel. She was about to make her way to Albert when she turned around again and asked in the haughtiest tone she could manage, "What are you going to show me?"

"You'll have to meet me on Sunday to see."

"No, seriously?"

He looked over his shoulder at her again. "Seriously. Gazebo. Not that I don't have all week to remind you."

"What?"

"I already followed you around today." He shrugged. "Might as well see the whole thing through."

Her eyebrows came together. "I didn't say yes."

"But you will," he said confidently.

"What makes you think I'll say yes just because you brought a couple cans of paint?"

Before he could reply, Natasha walked away, feeling triumphant.

While the boys were putting the finishing touches on the lemonade stand Thursday afternoon, Natasha started on the baking. Unlike the first time she had seen it, the kitchen was now spotless. No half-eaten food or empty boxes of takeout lying around. That was good. She placed all the ingredients on the counter and set about preheating the oven and searching for bowls, measuring cups, spatulas, and baking pans.

The stove and fridge were all stainless steel. The pots and pans were copper-bottom. The countertops were granite. And the cabinets were a cheery light maple.

"Hello, Natasha," Mrs. Winchester said as she entered the kitchen.

Natasha straightened from bending over one of the lower drawers, a whisk in her hand. "Mrs. Winchester, it's very good to see you."

Albert's mother regarded Natasha with silent assessment. Her eyes didn't seem puffy. And she did seem to have herself pulled together in a simple sweaterdress. But there were definite dark circles under her eyes that the concealer couldn't completely hide. She sat down on the counter and folded her hands on top of each other.

"I'm sorry I couldn't meet you at the door the day you came with the groceries," she said.

Natasha glanced over her shoulder while she preheated the oven. Mrs. Winchester couldn't quite maintain eye contact. She would feel the same way if anyone but Nathan, Caleb, or Didi had seen her sobbing her eyes out.

"Albert was the perfect host," Natasha replied as she stood to her full height.

"I appreciate what you did. Cleaning the kitchen. And now Albert tells me you're helping him with his project."

"He's such a great kid." Natasha smiled. "He's actually with Jackson right now. I think they're just about done with the lemonade stand."

"Yes. I saw them on my way here," she said, relief on her beautiful yet tired face. "I had no idea he was back in town. Are you two back together?"

The breath in Natasha's lungs froze. "No. He's just helping out."

Mrs. Winchester's lips curved upward. "It's been weeks since I saw my son smile so widely. Of course, he's getting paint everywhere, but it's a small price I'm willing to pay for his happiness."

Hearing that Jackson might have been responsible for making Albert happy did funny things to Natasha's heart. But she pushed those feelings aside. He had no right taking up so much space in her thoughts.

"That's good," Natasha said, returning her attention to the dry ingredients laid out before her. "I'm working on the cookies for tomorrow."

"I love the lemonade stand idea," Mrs. Winchester said. "When Samuel was alive, he could drink a pitcher of my lemonade on a hot summer day. It was the perfect combination of sweet and sour, he would say. The look on his face while he savored each sip made me feel like I saved the world by making him that drink."

Her wistful expression called to a familiar yearning in Natasha. "You miss him."

"Do you miss breathing?"

Natasha met Mrs. Winchester's gaze. "What do you mean?"

"Samuel may not be here with me anymore, but I carry him around here." Albert's mother tapped the center of her chest, then her temple. "And here. I remember him like I remember to breathe."

Mrs. Winchester squared her shoulders. In an instant, she seemed a decade younger. It was like a ray of sunshine had broken through the gray storm clouds, promising a new day.

"Thank you," she said. "Today is the first time that I feel like this house is coming back to life." Her smile was soft and from the heart. "You made it happen."

Natasha dropped her gaze, a flush pinking her cheeks. "I did nothing."

Albert's mom merely smiled before she stood up and walked out of the kitchen. Natasha wondered if a love like the Winchesters' was unique to them or if she'd ever experience it too. Then she remembered she'd had a love like theirs. One made for the movies. Or at least she'd thought so at the time.

Eleven

ENTREPRENEURSHIP DAY. A fun day for kids to sell their stuff. During their Entrepreneurship Day many years ago, all Jackson wanted was to help Natasha and Nathan sell out their glittery Valentine's cards. Now Jackson saw it more as the school trying to teach kids the value of money and the importance of business in a way that wasn't dry and boring. If little Chaz and Chip were to take over their families' companies someday, then they should start before they even hit puberty.

As soon as Jackson walked into the gym, the memories of his and his friends' exploits during Entrepreneurship Day came to mind. The basketball court had been made to look like a bazaar, with booths and stalls of all kinds. Kids as young as eight sold their wares to everyone invited to attend—mostly family and friends. Jackson collected no less than six kisses on the cheek that day. That was before high school. Way before Natasha started being more than just a friend. It was right after she returned home from a summer in Europe with breasts, to be exact.

What he remembered most about Entrepreneurship Day was the song of the chaos. His classmates running around, wide smiles on their faces. The murmur and chatter of the adults. Cheerful greetings from the sellers. And the slight hum in the background he couldn't quite identify. It was a glorious day. He probably still had the recording somewhere in his files.

Unfortunately, the experience today was different for Jackson. It seemed like he had cotton in his ears. The farther into the gym he got, the less he heard the cacophony of sounds. It was useless to pull his phone out and record. There was no hearing the results later anyway. His heart ached and his shoulders felt heavy. Maybe coming wasn't such a good idea. But he'd promised Albert. Backing out seemed like a douche move. Albert was counting on him. And he had to admit to being curious about seeing the final product of all their hard work.

Jackson was about to keep moving in search of the Wizarding World of Lemonade stand when he spotted Natasha in a pretty pink dress and sandals heading over to him. They locked gazes, and for the briefest second before she reached him the lines of a new song came to him. Something he hadn't heard in a while: an upbeat melody.

His heart punched hard against the cage of his chest. He lost his breath. For the first time in six months, he actually wanted to compose dance music again.

"What are you doing here?" Natasha demanded.

Under the gym lights, her eyes seemed bluer than usual. And

her hair. The strands were like a dark waterfall over her shoulders. The urge to reach out and touch her was strong.

The sound was gone. He was back to hearing the muffled noise surrounding them. But there were still echoes in his soul. Pure. Calling out to him. Where had they come from?

A knot formed on her brow. "Jax!"

He blinked twice, forcing himself to focus. "What?"

"What do you mean, 'what'?" She frowned.

"Look," he said with a sigh. "As much as I love seeing you, I'm actually here for Albert. In case you've forgotten, I worked hard on that lemonade stand. And my hands still sting from squeezing all those lemons."

"Excuse me, it was a group effort."

"I just want to check on our guy."

"UGH! Fine." She grabbed his wrist and pulled him along.

Liking the feel of her soft hand way too much, Jackson went along. Trailing in her wake gave him the best view of her backside. Not to mention every time he inhaled, his lungs were happy. She smelled of apples today.

Then she stopped abruptly. Jackson had to dig in his feet to keep from colliding with her. He'd learned that lesson from when they were at the art supply store. They weren't in the touching-and-getting-close stage yet.

"Why'd we stop?" he asked.

"Just look at him," she said.

Jackson followed her gaze to where Albert sat in his special lemonade stand. He had his arms crossed and wore a sad expression on his face. The stand itself looked great. The gold and crimson colors stood out. The sign that hung above was perfect. At the left post of the cardboard window cutout was the menu, with the prices of each item Albert was selling. Unfortunately, there was one key element missing.

There was no one buying any of his lemonade. The cookies and cupcakes were ignored as well. And in a gym filled with kids who lived for a sugar high? Not paying attention to the veritable feast of sweets was totally unacceptable.

"How long has it been like this?" Jackson asked, his chest heavy.

"Since we started," Natasha explained. "We finished setting up. Albert was so excited. I told him I was here if he needed me. He said he could take care of everything, so I kept my distance. Still hovering, of course, but I wanted to give him a chance."

"He even dressed up as Harry. That's commitment."

"But no one is buying any lemonade."

"We have to do something." Jackson surveyed the scene before them.

"Yeah, but no matter how hard I try to encourage kids to go and buy a glass or a cookie or cupcakes, none of them would listen to me. I'm at my wit's end here."

A ping of inspiration struck Jackson almost as soon as Natasha finished speaking. "When I'm spinning at a party, there's always some resistance at first."

"What does selling lemonade have to do with being a DJ?" She scowled at him.

He grinned, taking her annoyance in stride. "All I do is find one willing participant to kick things off. I zero in on that person and cater my beats to his or her moves. Pretty soon the crowd follows."

"I still don't understand."

Reaching into his back pocket, Jackson pulled out a dollar from his wallet.

Natasha watched as Jackson neared Albert. The boy lost his frown for a second when he recognized who had arrived. They spoke, and Albert's frown returned. Natasha had a feeling the boy was explaining his predicament. Jackson listened intently, stuffing one hand into the pocket of his jeans. He nodded and agreed with everything Albert said. Then he pointed at one of the pitchers of lemonade—the red one that was meant to represent Gryffindor. They had green, blue, and yellow too, for the other houses.

Albert eagerly poured Jackson a cup. Jackson handed him a dollar and took a sip. He smiled, then said something that made Albert laugh. Then Jackson ambled away.

At first, Natasha had no idea what he was doing until he reached the center of the basketball court. He took another sip of the red lemonade, then said in a voice loud enough for anyone near him to hear, "Wow! This is great!" He looked so cool in his leather jacket, T-shirt, jeans, and boots that kids turned to stare at him.

A minute passed. Nothing.

But by the time Jackson was halfway done with his glass, six kids approached him. A boy with curly brown hair led the pack. He looked up at Jackson and said, "You're DJ Ax, right?"

Jackson grinned. "Yup."

"Cool," the kids said in chorus.

Then the leader spoke rapidly. "I watched your videos on YouTube. They were awesome."

"Thank you." Jackson raised his cup of lemonade.

The kids all looked at him, and one of them asked, "What's that?"

"Oh, this?" Jackson pointed at the cup. "It's the best lemonade in here. You can get it at that booth."

He pointed toward Albert's booth. Almost immediately, the group turned on their heels and ran for the lemonade stand.

A smile started small on Natasha's lips until it stretched wide and reached her eyes. She finally understood what Jackson had done. He knew that at least a few kids would recognize him, and that was more than enough incentive to copy what he was doing. Albert happily sold lemonade and cookies, a big smile on his face for the first time that day.

Taking her cue from Jackson, Natasha purchased a cup for herself and mingled among the crowd. Every time she stopped at a booth or chatted with an assembled group, she casually mentioned how great the lemonade from that Harry Potter stand was. Pretty soon Albert was inundated with kids and grown-ups who wanted a taste, and a line formed.

"You were right," Natasha said as she joined Jackson at the bleachers. She sat down on the first rung while Jackson remained standing. "All it takes is one and the rest will follow. And it doesn't hurt if that one is mildly famous."

He smiled. "It doesn't hurt that we made damn good lemonade," he said after finishing his second cup. "No one can deny a great product. That plus word of mouth will always win. And what exactly do you mean by 'mildly'?"

Natasha pressed her lips together to keep from smiling. The last thing she wanted was to give him the satisfaction. Instead she asked, "Why do you know so much about this?"

He shrugged, keeping his gaze on the line and Albert

interacting with each new customer. "It's what happened with my music. I focused on making the best product that I could be proud of. Then it took getting the track in the right hands. One recommendation turned into ten, and ten turned into a hundred. The next thing I know I'm waking up to news that my songs are climbing the charts."

"It sounds like a dream the way you talk about it."

"Sometimes I have to pinch myself just to see if I'll wake up."

Natasha cradled her cup in both hands, swirling the blue lemonade around and around. "If it was going so well, then why did you come back?"

Jackson inhaled sharply, as if the question had caught him unawares. Then he let out his breath slowly. She looked up at him, not sure what to expect. His expression remained neutral when he finally spoke.

"How many of my new songs have you heard?"

She opened her mouth to speak, but she wasn't exactly sure how to respond. So she paused and thought about it. Was he fishing for compliments?

"A couple," she said nonchalantly.

He gave her a sidelong glance. "Heard any from the last six months?"

"Jackson, my life doesn't revolve around downloading your next hit."

"That's the problem," he said. Then he let out a long, hard sigh—the kind that seemed to move through his entire body. "My last couple of songs are total flops. According to the few people who *did* listen to them, they were sad. Sappy. Heartbreakingly mediocre."

Her shoulders tensed. "What? Why? You write dance music."

"Exactly." He barked a sad laugh. "It happened after Amsterdam."

"So you're blaming this on me."

"Of course not." He rubbed his forehead before looking her in the eye. "I'm just telling you what happened. From the beginning, all my music was about you. About how happy I was that we were together. When you left me in Amsterdam, everything went south in my songwriting. I missed you so much that it showed in my music. Then I realized that without you in my life, there's no music."

Everything in Natasha screamed that she should be pissed. Was he seriously making his successes and failures about her? Yet she couldn't deny the fact that when he said his songs were about her, heat spread across her face. Then she saw the briefest flicker of hurt in Jackson's expression.

"I . . . I don't know what to say," she whispered, not trusting herself to speak louder for fear that her voice would break.

"Say you'll meet me at the gazebo on Sunday." He returned his gaze to Albert. "Please, Tash. Let me make it up to you. I made a mistake letting you go. Let me show you that I'm serious about asking for your forgiveness."

Still affected by his admission, Natasha turned her gaze toward the lemonade stand. She mentally cataloged Albert's supply. The pitchers had been refilled. The cupcakes were selling. But the cookies seemed to be running low.

"He looks like he's really enjoying himself," Jackson said, changing the topic.

She nodded. At least Albert had found his purpose. Maybe she'd find hers soon.

"I guess you more than earned me showing up on Sunday," she said.

A grin flashed over Jackson's face. He seemed less tired than on the night of the engagement party.

"Admit it, there's definitely a thaw there," he teased.

"There is no thaw. No thaw at all." She kept her tone icy to prove the point. "I'm just being civil."

"There's a thaw."

She twisted in her seat and faced him, giving in to her curiosity. "What's going to happen on Sunday? Why do I have to be at the gazebo?"

"At five minutes before noon. Remember. That's the important part."

"Five minutes before noon," she repeated.

Twelve

SUNDAY COULDN'T COME fast enough for Natasha. A part of her was excited. It was hard to deny it. What did Jackson want to show her? He seemed adamant that she meet him. She was willing to hear him out and meet him since he'd helped Albert, but showing up didn't mean she was ready to forgive him. Not by a long shot.

Yet the other part of her was afraid. Maybe he had been right. Had there really been a thaw? She should have accounted for the fact that Jackson was as stubborn as she was. It was as if the more she pushed back, the more he clung to the idea that maybe he had a chance. Did he?

As she parked her SUV at a coffee shop about a block away, Natasha didn't even want to think about the possibility of forgiveness. But watching Jackson with Albert the other day made her forget his faults. And he had been careful with her, she could give him that much—conscious not to touch her, while staying close. She'd felt his eyes on her while he maintained a comfortable distance. Which was why she was curious.

The walk to the town square didn't help clear her confused mind. She was there because she never backed out when she said she would do something. Let him show her whatever it was. How bad could it be?

She glanced at the watch on her wrist and walked faster. Two minutes left before the scheduled time of their meeting. Her heart kicked up its pace. Her breath grew shallow not from exertion but from the building anticipation that propelled her forward.

The Sunday crowd was thin and lazy. Most opted to stay home, relishing the last day of the weekend before work resumed the next day. Cars leisurely drove past. Even children seemed more subdued, devoid of their usual boisterous energy.

When the gazebo, with its flowering vines and wooden benches, came into sight, Natasha could barely breathe. Her dress seemed too tight and her sandals heavy. Her gaze searched as she moved forward. Once her eyes found Jackson standing at the center of the gazebo, her heart stopped.

He wore his usual leather jacket, T-shirt, and jeans. But what slayed her were the Ray-Ban aviator sunglasses shielding his eyes from the bright spring sun.

She knew the instant he turned his head and found her. It was as if an electric current danced over her skin. It was more than goose bumps. It was more intense than shivers. It was as if her entire body paid attention.

One hand in the pocket of his jeans, he reached out for her with the other. As if by silent command, her feet moved of their own volition. She didn't run. DoCo princesses didn't run.

Before crossing the street, she looked both ways. No oncoming cars. She stepped onto the road and sauntered her way to the gazebo. The steps creaked beneath her feet. Without thinking, she raised her hand to meet his still-outstretched one. But just as their palms were about to touch, she hesitated and pulled back.

Resisting the urge to bite the corner of her lower lip, she raised her chin and said, "Hi."

Jackson dropped his hand to his side. "Hi."

The electricity in the air between them was palpable. Natasha knew if they touched she might combust.

No longer comfortable looking at him without being able to read his eyes behind those dark lenses, she checked her watch. "I'm here. What happens next?"

"Just wait." Jackson looked up at the clock tower a few yards away from the gazebo. The small hand was pointing to the stylized number twelve while the long hand moved to the eleven, marking five minutes until noon.

So Natasha waited. And waited. Every few seconds she glanced at the clock tower, then her watch.

"Jackson, I still have stuff—"

"Shh," he said, interrupting her.

"What exactly is supposed to hap—"

Natasha stopped speaking on her own. Her gaze traveled to the sidewalk opposite the gazebo. She could have sworn the people were walking not a minute ago. Now they stood frozen. Then, in her periphery, she noticed something odd. She turned to her right to see that the cars on the road had stopped moving.

Slowly, she turned in a circle. The Sunday strollers were also frozen in place.

"How?" she whispered.

No one moved. Nothing moved. Even the shops surrounding them, previously bustling with activity, were still. The entire town square was quiet. Everything and everyone was suspended in time.

Wonder and awe flowing through her veins, Natasha completed her revolution to face Jackson again. He took her hands in his, and she let him because her mind wasn't working properly. It was so bizarre seeing the entire square so silent.

"Do you remember the time the clock tower was broken?" he asked softly, as if he didn't want to disturb the stillness.

She nodded, then swallowed. "Every time I passed it, I'd stop to check if they had fixed it."

The clock tower's bell tolled, breaking the silence. Natasha jumped back, startled. She clutched her chest in an attempt to keep her heart's hammering at bay. Her head swiveled from side to side.

With each new chime, it was as if the spell had been broken. First, the cars resumed driving. Next, the people started walking again. Then the shops came back to life. Dogs barked. Children played. By the last chime, she returned her gaze to Jackson, who was smiling from ear to ear.

Giddy, she asked, "How did you do that?"

"A magician never reveals his tricks."

"Jax!"

"All right." He sighed. "You know I can't say no when you look at me like that."

"That was the most amazing thing I've ever seen." She tugged at his jacket. "Come on, tell me."

"First, we cordoned off the town square. It was easy enough to do on a Sunday." He closed his hand on hers, and she didn't pull away. "Then we populated the entire area around the gazebo with this performance troupe I met in Las Vegas during a gig. I flew them in for this."

"They were all paid actors?"

He nodded. "Even the ones in the cars."

"That's why you wanted me here five minutes before noon."

"Made sense. It would be cruel to have them posing for longer than that." He paused to remove his sunglasses.

Staring into those bright golden eyes took Natasha's breath away. It was as if everything stopped once again. Time. Place. The universe itself.

Then he leaned forward. Natasha tensed, unsure what she should do. But instead of the kiss she thought was coming, Jackson whispered into her ear.

"Did I manage to stop time?"

His breath tickled, raising the hairs on the back of her neck. She was once again so aware of him. Of his scent. Of his height. Of his body heat. Yet the only place he touched her was the hand he held in his own.

"What are you doing?" she asked, voice shaky.

"I want you back," he said, plain and simple, as if he was accepting some challenge. "You can ignore me all you want. You can be mad at me. But you won't scare me off. I'm not leaving. I'm not giving up until you forgive me."

Unable to take the assault on her senses and with her mind running on overdrive, Natasha pulled her hand out of his grasp and stepped away.

"Tash?"

"I-I have to go," she stammered. The floor beneath her seemed unstable.

"Wait." He took a step toward her.

"Jax, stop."

He did. Confusion crossed his features. She knew the question in his gaze, which, unfortunately, she had no answer for.

Instead she willed her legs to work. She had to get as far away from him as she possibly could.

Jackson stood in the gazebo long after Natasha left. For a second there, he'd thought he had her. The amazement in her eyes was priceless. And she smelled so good. Strawberry.

Then she ran away. He expected the resistance. It was too easy if she gave in right away. But there were lingering feelings. It was in the confusion that appeared in her expression before she thought to mask it with something else. But it seemed like he needed to go bigger. Stopping time wasn't enough. He had to think of another way to show her he was serious.

After paying the actors and making sure the town square was opened to the public again, Jackson rode home more determined than ever.

When he arrived at the manor, he went straight to his bedroom. Already his mind was working, lining up options. Maybe some time searching on the Internet might help?

He padded to his desk, where his laptop sat open. His gaze

landed on the MIDI controller he used to compose dance tracks. If he closed his eyes, he was sure he could conjure up the melody of watching Natasha as he'd stopped time. She was the embodiment of a song. Yet as soon as he heard the first few notes, they faded away.

Frustrated, he pulled back his desk chair and sat down. He opened a web browser and typed *defying gravity* in the search bar. Upon pressing Enter, he was directed to a song from a hit Broadway play.

"Not that kind of defying gravity," he mumbled to himself as he tried again with *defy gravity*.

The search netted several interesting results, two of which were more promising than most. The first was a trampoline park. But he quickly rejected the idea. He wanted something bigger than that.

His eyes scanned through the many links until his gaze fell on a website that offered skydiving at the local airport. At first, he was hesitant to click on the link. It wasn't exactly defying gravity. It was more like falling. But during his world tour, he'd been lucky enough to experience skydiving multiple times. There was a moment where you were free-falling. That was as close to defying gravity as it was going to get, he thought.

Then a memory came to mind. It was during the Fourth of July party at the lake a couple of years back. He and Natasha had watched as skydivers with red, white, and blue smoke coming out of their packs performed aerial maneuvers. Jackson had his arms around Natasha. In her excitement, she was bouncing in place. She looked up at him and said she wanted to skydive someday. With him.

Anyone else would have thought that Natasha was joking or making an empty promise. But not Jackson. He knew the look of determination in her eyes.

He rubbed his chin and read through the website. How could he convince her to go with him? After she'd left him at the gazebo that morning, her reluctance might be tougher to crack. He had to get creative.

A smile stretched across his face. Jackson was nothing if not creative.

Right away he knew just the person who could help. He fished out his phone and made the call.

Thirteen

FOR THE REST of the week, the only thing on Natasha's mind was Jackson stopping time for her. One minute, her heart was melting. The next she paced her room in anger, accusing him of manipulating her emotions just so she would forget what he'd done. Well, she was never going to forget, she reminded herself. That was right about the time she began having arguments with herself like a crazy person.

So, by Friday, when the invitation from Didi came to have lunch, Natasha leapt at the chance to get out of the house to see a friendly face. She was so excited that she arrived way too early at the cute little café Caleb had taken her to last summer when he interned for his father's law firm. She loved the baby-blue-and-powder-white-polka-dot wallpaper and the butter-yellow upholstery on the chairs.

While she waited at a corner table, caught up in her own thoughts, the ringtone of the girl sitting with her friends at a table next to hers startled her. It was one of Jackson's songs.

Hearing it immediately brought her back to the night Jackson took her to Diablo. It was a club an hour outside of town, where he was the resident DJ on Fridays when he was first starting out. That night was the first time he invited her to watch him play.

Natasha made sure to use Jackson's body as a shield against the crush of people inside the club as they made their way to the raised booth at the far end of the dance floor. A guy with headphones on was bobbing to the music while his hands flew over the turntable in front of him.

Jackson approached the DJ and tapped his shoulder. Then he whispered into the DJ's ear. The guy nodded, and Jackson set up his gear. In swift, practiced movements, Jackson pulled his laptop out from his pack, hung earphones around his neck, and replaced the vinyl discs on the turntables with several new ones. He adjusted the knobs and dials as the crowd cheered, recognizing him.

Natasha sucked in a breath as the force of their adoration hit her. The screams—from both men and women—were a wall of sound hitting her in waves over and over again. They had their arms raised. Some were taking pictures. Others were shouting that they loved Jackson. That they wanted to marry him.

Jackson concentrated on his setup. Once he was ready, he took the mic from the other DJ and addressed the crowd.

"Are you ready?" Jackson asked.

The crowd screamed in response.

"I said, are you *ready*?" He pointed the mic toward the

crowd, and the audience screamed even louder. "Then let's dance."

Jackson put on his headphones and pressed Enter on his laptop. A second later, a raging beat filled the club. It was fast like a laser, ending in an explosive downbeat. Then his fingers twisted knobs on the wide board in front of him. The bass turned up.

Natasha flicked her gaze from Jackson to the dance floor. Every body moved in time with the music. Hips swayed. Hands waved. Heads bobbed. It was magic the way one twist of a knob or push of a button controlled the movements of those below the booth. She had never seen anything like it.

Breathless, Natasha returned her attention to Jackson.

It was surreal watching him take command of a room with just a laptop and the sliding and turning of dials on a massive soundboard. Her brain couldn't comprehend how he was putting the notes together, making the act seem like child's play. Yet somehow she could tell he was feeling the mood of the crowd and acting accordingly. It was as if he was choreographing their actions with his music.

A confusing mix of pride and envy swirled in her chest. She was proud of what he had accomplished in such a short time. It was amazing. She allowed her body to feel the beat. Soon she was swaying, turning, and shaking her hips. Then she heard her voice through the speakers in time with the music.

Natasha froze.

Jackson looked over his shoulder at her. He pressed another button on his laptop and the words became clear.

"I love you," she said. But it was more like she was singing than speaking. "I will love you forever and ever."

She couldn't recall when she had said those words while being recorded. Jackson's hand circled her wrist. In the next instant, she was pulled in front of the turntable with his arms on either side of her body.

Her face burned at the closeness. But she couldn't allow herself to be swept up. She needed to know, so she turned in his arms. Placing a hand on his shoulder for support, she stood on tiptoe, pulled back one earphone, and asked, "What was that about?"

A hand on her hip turned her back around. Before she could protest, lips touched the shell of her ear. Then Jackson whispered, "Do you remember that afternoon by the lake? I was recording you in the water, splashing around."

If she thought her face couldn't get any hotter, she was wrong. She remembered. It was one of the happiest days of her life. She couldn't quite recall what she had been happy about. But she remembered Jackson pulling out his phone and her telling him that she loved him.

She gasped. The heat from his body. The feeling of being surrounded. It was all too much. It took all that was left of her concentration to focus on his question as she grabbed the edge of the soundboard for support.

"All the songs I create, all the lyrics I write, are about you."

Instant pain rushed across Natasha's chest, bringing her back to the present. The corners of her eyes stung. If his songs were about her, then how could he throw away what they had?

"Am I late?" Didi asked. Then the smile on her face froze. "Are you all right?"

Natasha discreetly dabbed at her eyes and stood up,

sniffing loudly for effect. "I just got here," she lied. "And my allergies are acting up." Another lie, since she didn't have allergies. But when in a pinch . . .

She and Didi hugged before sitting down. A server approached them with menus.

"Are you sure you're okay?" Didi asked again after they gave their orders.

"I'm fine," Natasha insisted. But she also knew that if she wanted to survive her confusion in one piece, she needed to confide in her friends. "I'm just suffering through a full-court press from Jackson."

"Okay, sports term. You've lost me."

"Jackson isn't just back in town. He's back because he's determined that I forgive him for leaving." When Natasha took a deep breath, her shoulders rose. "Last Sunday he stopped time for me."

Didi scratched her head. "Okay, officially confused."

Natasha launched into an abbreviated version of Jackson's visit to her room the night of the engagement party. Didi laughed at the flower regifting incident, but her expression turned serious when Natasha reached the part where she said that time would have to stop—among other conditions—before she would even consider forgiving him. Then she explained what had happened at the gazebo by the clock tower.

Fanning her face, Didi sat back in her chair. "Wow. Just wow."

"Will you please not be on his side about this?"

"Who says I'm on his side?"

"The look of utter awe on your face right now?"

Didi pushed her eyebrows together in a mock imitation of a stern expression. Natasha rolled her eyes and shook her head the second she felt her lips quirk up.

"You know what I mean," Natasha said after she was sure she wasn't going to laugh.

"Tash, I'm on your side." Didi reached across the table and gave Natasha's hand a reassuring squeeze. "But you also have to admit that what he did was pretty cool. That's a doozy of a grand gesture."

"Who said anything about grand gestures?"

"Come on." Didi eyed her. "What he did was straight out of the movies."

Natasha slumped into her chair in a most unladylike fashion. "That's what I was afraid of. I'm just not ready to forgive him."

"But there have to be some feelings left there, right?"

"Didi, you know as well as anyone that when you love someone that much, those feelings don't just go away, even if he does something unforgivable. We were together for so long, I don't even remember a time without Jackson in my life. Even when we were growing up, I knew there was already something between us. It was just a matter of making it official."

"Nathan told me your parents were practically planning the wedding."

Natasha sighed wistfully. "I honestly thought he was my forever, you know?"

A pretty blush swept over Didi's cheeks. "I know."

Before Natasha could say anything else, their food arrived. She and Didi quickly lapsed into talking about other things, like Didi's upcoming show and how Nathan couldn't resist helping out. If there was a party that needed planning, her brother sensed it and came to the rescue.

Nathan being busy meant his focus wasn't all on Natasha, which she was secretly thankful for. Even after telling Didi about her Jackson concerns, it felt like she was back to square one in figuring out what to do.

By the end of their meal, Caleb waltzed in. Natasha welcomed the added distraction her cousin presented. At the same time, her heart ached at how attentive he was being toward Didi. Jackson used to be the same way. He always found a way to touch her, make her feel adored, even when he was speaking to someone else. He never gave all his attention to anyone else when Natasha was by his side.

"Tash, are you listening?"

Caleb's question knocked Natasha back to the present. Good thing too, because she was stepping right back into sentimental thoughts where Jackson was concerned.

"I'm sorry, I was distracted," she said. "What were you saying?"

Caleb smirked at catching her not paying attention before he repeated, "I won a certificate for a free skydiving lesson, and I don't know what to do with it."

Natasha's ears perked up. "Skydiving?"

"Yeah," he said. "It's for this weekend only, and I honestly don't have the time."

"I've always wanted to skydive."

"Really?" Caleb looked shocked. "Well, do you want it?"

"Sure!" The more she thought about the chance to jump out of a plane, the better the experience sounded in her head.

Maybe the high altitude would knock some sense into her. She had Jackson on the brain and she wanted him out.

"Are you sure about this, Tash?" Didi asked. "It sounds dangerous."

"I think a little danger is exactly what I need right now," Natasha said.

Fourteen

NATASHA SPENT ALL her time studying everything she could find on the Internet about skydiving. Finally, something to preoccupy herself with that didn't involve Jackson. It was a welcome relief.

Since it was her first dive, she would be going on a tandem skydive. According to the site, she was going to be strapped to a jumpmaster, and all she had to do was enjoy the ride. Her heart skipped a beat. Excitement revved through her veins.

Saturday morning she woke up bright and early. Since it was early May, the air still had a nip to it. The website said to dress comfortably, so Natasha opted for thermal leggings, a sweater, and the sneakers she'd worn when she helped Albert with his lemonade stand.

And just like that she was thinking of Jackson again. More

than a little frustrated that he kept worming his way into her head, as she drove to the drop zone Natasha pushed memories of him away and concentrated on the fun she would have.

Armed with the certificate Caleb had given her, Natasha practically skipped to the reception desk of Dodge Cove Skydivers. The woman at the desk happily greeted her, accepted the certificate, and made a call on her phone. Two minutes later, a man in a T-shirt and cargo shorts came up to her with a huge smile. He introduced himself as Lambert and said that he would be her jumpmaster that morning. They shook hands.

"Natasha Parker," she said, returning his smile with a giddy one of her own. "It's nice to meet you."

"I take it this is your first time, Natasha?" he asked, gripping his hips with his hands. He had such a confident air about him that it calmed some of her nervousness. She guessed he would have to be confident, since he jumped out of planes for a living.

"I've always wanted to skydive. I was just too busy to actually do anything about it earlier."

"Well, you've picked the right day. The weather is perfect for jumping out of a plane. Are you nervous?"

"More excited than nervous."

"Great." He hiked his thumb over his shoulder. "Let's go over to the orientation room. There is a video you will watch about what to expect. Then afterward we have some waivers to sign. After that, we're good to go."

Natasha gulped. That nervousness Lambert mentioned seemed to return at the mention of waivers. Of course, jumping out of a plane required those. Her legs wobbled slightly when she followed after Lambert, but she was still as excited as ever.

An hour later, Natasha was ready to go. Unfortunately, some of her excitement was eaten up by how uncomfortable the harness was. There were two straps on her shoulders and two on her chest, restricting her breathing. And when she walked, she had a perpetual wedgie. Not cool at all.

"Is it supposed to be this tight?" she asked as she and Lambert, who seemed so comfortable in his harness, walked toward a small plane.

"Wouldn't want you falling out, now would we?" Lambert joked.

"Not funny."

"After you." Lambert gestured toward the door of the plane.

Feeling her excitement and nervousness mingle into a single ball, Natasha gritted her teeth and climbed in. Instead of front-facing seats, the plane was retrofitted with benches running along both sides of the body. She picked one of the benches while Lambert sat across from her. The second the door was closed, the plane's engine sputtered to life and they were rolling down the runway.

Everything was happening so fast that Natasha didn't think of backing out until the plane's nose slanted upward and they were off the ground. Not once did her dive instructor lose his smile. He must have seen all kinds of first-time divers.

Not knowing what to do with her shaking hands, Natasha gripped her harness until her knuckles turned white. The sound of the plane zipping through the air was so loud that she could barely hear the pounding heart in her chest. Whether that was a good thing or a bad thing, she couldn't decide.

"Are you nervous yet?" Lambert asked as he strapped a GoPro camera to his forehead.

"Wait." A thought had occurred to Natasha that almost instantly made her forget she was getting a little scared. "How are you going to film this if I'm strapped to your chest? Won't the back of my head block the view?"

"Who said anything about you being strapped to me?"

"What?" Natasha's heart leapt to her throat. "I thought this was a tandem dive."

"It is," Lambert said casually. Then his gaze shifted toward the front of the plane.

"You'll be strapped to me," said a voice she recognized even through the roaring of the plane.

"You've got to be joking," Natasha said, feeling her stomach flip, as Jackson—wearing an all-black dive suit and harness—eased out of the copilot's seat and made his way to the bench she sat on. "What the hell are you doing here?"

"You always said you wanted to try skydiving," Jackson said as if they were having a normal conversation, when clearly they weren't because Natasha was seconds away from murdering him.

"I'm not doing this," she said, shaking her head. "The second we land, I'm going to kill Caleb. I should have known him winning the certificate was too good to be true." She sandwiched the word *winning* in air quotes.

"If you're going to be mad, be mad at me." Jackson faced her fully on the bench. "He was just helping me out. I knew you wouldn't have gone if the suggestion came from me."

She narrowed her gaze. "Is Didi in on this?"

"Caleb probably already filled her in, but she has nothing to do with this. It's all on me."

Anger erasing her previous nervousness, she returned her

gaze to Lambert, who was still smiling. "I want this plane on the ground, right now!"

"No can do." The dive instructor shook his head. "We're three minutes away from jumping."

When Jackson attempted to hold her hand, Natasha yanked it away so hard her knuckles almost hit her in the face.

"Don't touch me," she growled so harshly that Jackson actually eased back an inch. "How dare you use skydiving against me?"

"I'm not," he reassured her, keeping his voice calm. "I just want you to experience something you've always wanted to do."

"Then why can't I be strapped to him?" She pointed at Lambert.

"Because I'll be filming the experience," Lambert explained.

"Tash, I know you're mad. And you can continue being mad. But don't let being mad ruin the experience for you."

"You being here already did that, thank you very much." She crossed her arms and looked away. Puffy clouds zipped by out the window. Her heart skipped.

They were above the clouds. They would be falling through them. It was a chance of a lifetime. The sun was shining. The sky was so blue.

"All right," Jackson said solemnly. "If you really want to land, we'll land."

"No," she finally said.

"No?" Jackson and Lambert said in unison.

She sighed, letting go of some of her anger. She could continue hating Jackson after they landed on the drop zone, but she wasn't going to miss out on this experience just because he was here. Instead of looking at Jackson, she turned her attention to Lambert.

"Is he qualified to do this?" she asked. The last thing she wanted was to die in Jackson's hands.

"You two will be fine," Lambert said. "And I'll be there to help. There are two chutes in his pack." Then he glanced at the contraption on his wrist. "Jax, we're at eight thousand feet."

"We're going to strap in now," Jackson said as he eased closer to Natasha.

"O-okay," she managed to say around the heart beating in her throat as she turned her back toward Jackson.

With swift movements, he attached her harness to his. The series of snaps seemed so loud to her ears. The cabin of the plane was chilly, but being so close to Jackson almost made Natasha sweat. Her previously forgotten nervousness returned, but for an entirely different reason. He smelled so good. Damn it! Would it have killed him not to shower and stink so she could hate him more?

"Ten thousand feet," Lambert said, easing the door open. The roar of the plane and the air grew almost deafening.

"Okay, we're moving to the door," Jackson said against her ear as he waddled his way to the opening.

"Jackson, I'm scared," she said, for a moment forgetting all the hurt and pain he'd caused her, as they reached the door.

"Don't worry." He covered her tight fists with one hand while he balanced himself against a handhold with the other. "You're the bravest girl I know. You can do this. Just think of it like defying gravity."

The instant those two words clicked inside Natasha's head, Jackson was helping her cross her arms. Remembering her training, she lifted her feet so she hung against him and laid her head on his shoulder. The second the drop zone came into view, Lambert yelled, "Go!" and Natasha was falling out of the plane.

Jackson let out an earsplitting whoop at about the same time a scream leapt out of Natasha's chest. They were tumbling until Jackson righted them. He tapped Natasha on the shoulder, the signal for her to go into touch-down position. She bent her legs and kept her feet between Jackson's legs. As she was about to open her arms, Jackson closed his hands around her fists and stretched their arms out together.

"I'm flying," Natasha yelled in delight, but her words were stolen by the wind zipping past them.

Lambert zoomed their way and took her hands before giving her a thumbs-up. She returned the gesture, smiling so wide that air was getting in between her teeth and cheeks. It wasn't a pretty look, and the camera was capturing every second of it, but she didn't care. She was skydiving!

She had the most amazing view of Dodge Cove. She could practically see the entire town below her, even the man-made lake in the distance and the roofs of the houses surrounding it. She whooped. Happiness to the extreme filled her insides.

Then, with a sudden jerk, she was tugged upward. She screamed again, but with joy instead of fright. The parachute unfurled above them. Soon they were landing on the ground.

The second Jackson released her from the harness strapping them together, Natasha turned around and hugged him. When she pulled back, she stared into his eyes, as bright as her own. Blood pumping, ears ringing, she took his face in her hands, shifted all her weight to her toes, and kissed him.

At first, Jackson stood frozen, as if every muscle in his body had gone rigid. She could actually feel his tension. Then, like ice melting under the summer sun, he wrapped one arm around her waist and cupped the back of her head with his other hand. She willingly pressed herself against him.

The rush of falling and being with him as it happened carried her away. She ran the tip of her tongue against his lips. He opened for Natasha, giving her what she needed. The taste of him was as she remembered. It might be the adrenaline coursing through her veins, but she couldn't get enough. She had to have more. So she kissed him and kissed him until she was left gasping and light-headed.

When she broke the kiss, she said, "That was amazing."

At first Jackson seemed confused, and then he said, "You are amazing."

Their gazes held for a hot minute. So much emotion swirled within Jackson's golden gaze. There was so much truth there. His feelings for her. His determination to win her back. All that he was. He circled her waist with his arms, not allowing her an inch of space.

Lambert's howl of excitement couldn't have come fast enough. The moment the instructor landed, it was like a lightbulb popping. Natasha's gut dropped. She'd kissed Jackson. In all the excitement she'd momentarily forgotten what he had done.

The panic forming in his expression told her he saw the realization and regret dawn on hers. She covered her open mouth with a hand. Needing to get out of there, she pushed out of Jackson's arms.

"I can't do this," she said, her hand muffling her voice.

With the last of her strength, she turned around and made a run for it.

"Tash, wait!" Jackson called after her, but she kept going, praying to anyone who would listen that he wouldn't come after her. That wasn't what she needed. He wasn't what she needed.

Oh God. She'd made a huge mistake.

Fifteen

JACKSON STOOD FROZEN in place as Natasha ran away . . . again. His first instinct was to run after her. Comfort her. But how could he comfort someone whose pain he had caused? A huge block of regret formed in his chest. Again and again, it seemed like no matter what he did, nothing turned out right, leaving him feeling like a failure. And his plans always seemed to upset the girl he loved even more in the process.

When she had kissed him, he was so sure taking her skydiving had been the right move. The feel of her against him. The scent of her. His whole body missed all of her. Yet seeing the hurt on her face when she realized what she had done shattered him into a million pieces. Was he being selfish continuing to pursue her?

She had kissed him. Chalk it up to the adrenaline, blinding

her from reality for a second. But the instant her lips touched his, she claimed him. Showed him that beneath all that anger and pain, she still had feelings for him. The confusion he felt was now magnified tenfold.

A hand on his shoulder broke him out of his daze. He gave Lambert a sidelong glance. The dive instructor was also looking in the direction Natasha had gone.

"Tough break, man," Lambert said.

Jackson sighed. "I'll make sure she returns the harness in case she actually drives off with it."

"For sure I thought you'd gotten her back when she kissed you," the dive instructor continued, stuck on the topic Jackson had tried to steer them away from.

"I thought so too," Jackson said, giving in. Then he packed up all the emotions into a small box inside him to think about later and faced Lambert fully. "Thanks anyway for letting me do this. I know I'm still a few dives short of officially leading a tandem dive."

"Consider it the first and last favor I do for you."

Jackson shook Lambert's hand, trying not to feel like he'd done all that for nothing.

Jackson was at a stoplight when his phone rang. He eased the bike to the side of the road to give the car behind him space to go and turned off the engine as he answered the call. Not bothering to check caller ID, he removed his helmet and brought the phone to his ear.

"Yeah," he said in a dejected tone.

"What the fuck is wrong with you?"

Caleb shouted so loudly from the other end of the call that

Jackson had to pull the receiver away. But the angry words didn't stop there.

"My cousin is with her brother right now, bawling her eyes out! What the hell happened?"

Dropping his head, Jackson ran his fingers through his hair as he said, "Meet me at the Lucky Duck in half an hour. You can continue screaming at me there."

The call went dead the second Jackson finished speaking. Heart like a lead ball in his chest, he slipped his phone back in his jeans pocket and kick-started his motorcycle.

The Lucky Duck was their favorite Chinese place. The restaurant sat right at the edge of downtown and was usually empty in the afternoons. Jackson knew the owner and apologized in advance for the ruckus he was sure Caleb was about to make.

Five minutes after Jackson was given their usual corner booth, Caleb strode in like he owned the place. He didn't have to search for Jackson; he knew where his friend would be, since they all ate at the same table whenever they craved Chinese. All of them—Caleb, the twins, Preston, and Jackson—had practically grown up at the Lucky Duck.

Without waiting for an invite, Caleb slid into the booth across from where Jackson sat and said, "When I agreed to help you with this skydiving stunt of yours, I thought I was on the side of love. Natasha had been sad without you. That's crystal clear. So I thought, why not help the guy out? He won't hurt her."

"I never planned on hurting her," Jackson said, already on the defensive. The words tasted foul in his mouth. He was man enough to admit when he'd messed up. But he wasn't going to sit there and just take it. "Not when I left. Not when I came back. Not when I set out getting her to forgive me."

"Well, that's just peachy, isn't it?" Caleb poked the table with his index finger so hard that if it was full of cutlery, they might have been clattering. "Now I have someone who I consider my sister hurt because of this stunt. I should never have gone through with this."

"Don't you think I feel the same way right now?"

"Bullshit. Hindsight is twenty-twenty."

Jackson leaned back, his shoulders falling. "I really messed up."

"Understatement of the century, pal."

"No." He lifted his gaze while keeping his head bowed. "I mean, I really hurt Tash. Like really bad, didn't I?"

"Einstein, that's what I've been saying from the beginning. What part of 'complete mess' didn't you understand when we talked before?"

Jackson stared at his hands on the table. "I thought I was fixing things." He covered his face with both hands, attempting to rub away the sadness that was spreading like wildfire inside him. "It's like no matter what I do, I'm just making more of a mess. I'm such an asshole."

"You got that right," Caleb said, but with less heat.

"What am I going to do?" Jackson asked, but to no one in particular.

Caleb raised a hand. In seconds a server was by his side. He ordered the dim sum platter and a pot of oolong tea.

Straightening in his seat, Jackson studied Caleb. "What are you doing?"

"When I called you," his friend began, "I was honestly

ready to bury you in the woods where no one was ever going to find you."

"At this point? I might even let you."

"But as shocking as this might be, I'm actually really impressed that you're going the distance for Tash."

"I never stopped loving her, man," Jackson said truthfully.

"Have you ever considered just leaving?"

Almost immediately, Jackson shook his head. "Not going to happen. I meant it when I told her I was here to stay."

"I figured." Caleb picked up one of the ceramic cups filled with hot tea that the server had left. "So what are you going to do now?"

Jackson picked up his own cup and let the heat from the ceramic seep into his skin. It settled the confusion inside of him enough that he could think clearly.

"It looks like grand gestures aren't working," he said, staring at the clear amber liquid with steam rising from the top.

"What tipped you off?"

Usually, he would have bitten Caleb's head off for his sarcasm, but Jackson knew quite well that he deserved it. He went through all the options in his head. There weren't very many left. Until he reached the most obvious conclusion.

He brought the cup to his mouth and took a bracing swallow of the hot tea. "It's time to call in the big guns."

Caleb's eyes grew wide. "Are you thinking what I think you're thinking?"

Jackson wasn't sure what his friend meant, so he said, "I'm going to bite the bullet and ask the help of the one person who knows Natasha better than anyone else."

"I was afraid you'd say that." Caleb shook his head in

admiration. "You've got a brass pair on you if you think Nathan will be willing to help after your latest stunt."

The wince was unstoppable. Jackson knew what he was facing. The wrath of Nathan Parker was legendary. He was nice to everyone until you give him a reason not to be. And Jackson had screwed up big-time.

"It's a long shot," he said, feigning confidence when really he was scared shitless. Caleb didn't have to know that.

"Maybe Tash just doesn't believe yet that you're here to stay," Caleb said in passing as the server returned with a huge tray filled with a dozen bamboo containers.

Jackson was taken aback by the words. Holy hell, how could he have missed the most obvious thing? Of course Natasha would doubt his sincerity. He'd never given her reason to believe otherwise.

With renewed determination, he picked up a pair of chopsticks and brought a spring roll to his mouth. He swallowed first before speaking.

"This meal's on me."

"Wouldn't have it any other way." Caleb grinned.

Sixteen

IT TURNED OUT a full stomach did help. Jackson stepped out of the Lucky Duck with Caleb feeling better than when he had come in. Halfway through their meal, Caleb had told him that Nathan was helping Didi with her art show that coming Wednesday. Jackson immediately made plans to attend the event and speak to Nathan then.

He was about to part ways with Caleb when his gaze wandered across the street to the closed music store. It was a beautiful two-story brick building. A group of people were gathered outside, looking up at the building.

"When did the music store close?" Jackson asked.

"Last year," Caleb said, hands in his pockets. "Probably a couple months after you left."

"I bought my first guitar there." Something in Jackson's gut told him to move. "Come on, let's take a look."

Jackson crossed the street without checking to see if Caleb was following him. One of the men in the group was explaining that the building was a great commercial space.

"Is that information about the building?" Jackson asked the man, pointing at the stack of paper with a picture of the building he was holding. "Can I have one?"

The man eyed Jackson for a second before giving him a flier. Then he returned his attention to the group, continuing his presentation.

"What are you doing?" Caleb whisper-hissed at Jackson's side.

"Aren't you curious to see what's inside?" Jackson stepped forward until he reached the door with its glass panel.

"No," Caleb said, but he followed after Jackson anyway.

They entered the wide-open space with its wood floors and brick walls. A thin coat of dust blanketed a lonely table in the corner and everything else, even the light fixtures above them.

"Wow, this place looks huge when it's empty." Jackson took the place in, then glanced at the information in his hands. There were several rooms on the second floor. The offices were on the first floor. "Look, there's a basement."

"Seriously, what is going on?" Caleb asked him just as the Realtor and the people with him entered the building as well.

Jackson ignored them all. There was a force driving him to look at the basement. He put one foot in front of the other until he reached a set of stairs that led down. The light was on, giving the entire area a soft glow. No fluorescent lighting anywhere, which Jackson immediately appreciated. He climbed down the stairs, listening to the sound his footsteps made bouncing off the walls.

"Whoa. The acoustics are amazing down here," Jackson said.

One wall was brick while the rest was left smooth. He was already imagining soundproofing options. The exposed pipes above them gave the space an edgy, underground feel.

"Jax." Caleb placed a hand on his shoulder. "Talk to me, man."

"Don't you think this space would make a great studio?"

In an instant, Jackson found the proof that he had been thinking about at the Lucky Duck. It killed two birds with one stone: that he would stay in DoCo and that his dream of starting his own studio would be realized. His gaze ran over the place. Already his mind was working on where everything went. There was enough space for several studios, a smaller one for voice recording and a larger one for bands. The possibilities were endless, limited only by his imagination.

"You're not seriously thinking of buying this place, are you?" Caleb asked him, awe on his face.

Jackson smiled as he fished out his phone and searched for his brother's number in his contacts list. Then he brought the receiver to his ear, waiting for the call to connect.

When it did, he said, "Hey, Bax, I'm at the old music store. Yes, the one downtown. I want to buy it."

He could make music anywhere. If she chose to leave, he would go with her. But if she chose to stay, then this was the only way he could show her that he was serious about being with her.

The ride home was exhilarating. It seemed like a weight had been lifted from Jackson's shoulders. The look on Caleb's face was priceless during the entire phone call it took to initiate the sale. Baxter said he would look into the particulars and get back to him Monday.

The second he got home, all Jackson wanted was to work. There was a melody that had settled into his brain the second he left the music store. But he was met by his mother. The concern on her face alerted him that something was up.

"Jackie, you have a guest waiting for you in the living room," she said.

"Everything okay, Mom?"

"You should go. Wouldn't want to keep your guest waiting." Her smile wobbled.

Jackson watched her leave before he turned toward the living room. His mother's concern was infectious, and he knotted his brow as he approached. Curling his fingers into the handholds, he pushed the sliding doors aside. On one of the couches sat the massive figure of his manager. He seemed so out of place in his wrinkled gray suit among all the sleek, classic lines of the room.

"Hutch, what the hell are you doing here?" Jackson asked.

Hutch pulled out a handkerchief from his inside pocket and dabbed at his forehead. "The break is over. I need you to get back to work."

Jackson stepped into the room and pulled the sliding doors closed behind him. His mother's concern made sense. Did she fear that he was leaving again?

"Do you know how many gigs I had to pass up in the name

of this 'break'?" Hutch continued. "And all the calls from reporters I had to dodge just for you? Asking about your next step. What happened. When your next single is coming out. Ambush interviews are par for the course, I get it. But at least make it worth my while by working."

Jackson's expression hardened. "It's all about the money for you, isn't it? It was never about the music."

"How naive are you?" Hutch's expression soured. "This isn't called the music business for nothing. I signed you because I saw the potential."

"To make money."

"Don't be a hypocrite. You come from a wealthy family. You don't even *need* this money. To you, this is all just for fun."

The realization that dawned on Jackson was a hard punch in the gut. He was surprised he was still standing on both feet.

"Is that why you worked me to the bone? Not caring if I slept or not? Sometimes booking two gigs in a night?"

"You enjoyed it."

"Get out." Jackson pointed at the door.

"Excuse me?" Hutch paled.

"I'm not your artist anymore."

"You signed a contract."

"Then you will be hearing from my lawyer." Jackson pushed the doors apart so hard they rattled in their hinges. "I'm not working for someone who ignores what I need to be happy. Get out before I toss you out."

"Jax, let's be reasonable about this," Hutch said, changing his tone.

Unable to look at Hutch a second longer, Jackson strode up to him, grabbed him by the collar of his suit, and dragged him to the front door. Hutch struggled, but Jackson held firm. He opened the door and shoved his manager out, shutting the door with a slam. Out of all the decisions he had made so far, none felt as satisfying as the one he had just made. It also meant another call to Baxter, but it could wait. He had a song to compose.

Seventeen

BY WEDNESDAY EVENING, Natasha had pulled herself back together enough to attend Didi's art show. Even if she was mad at Caleb for tricking her into going skydiving, it didn't mean she couldn't support Didi. And a part of her was glad to get out of the house. She no longer wanted to shut herself away just because something awful had happened.

Like kissing her ex.

"I'm so glad you could come," Didi said as they stood by the painting of Preston bathing in a giant tub of milk. It was weird. But it was so Didi.

"The event is packed," Natasha replied, squeezing her friend's arm. "I wouldn't miss this for the world."

"I promise you, if I'd known what Caleb was up to, I wouldn't have let him trick you into going skydiving."

Natasha shook her head. "Don't worry about it. I shouldn't have kissed Jackson, but I did. It's there. It happened. All I want is to move on." Even if thoughts of Jackson's mouth on hers made the hummingbirds in her stomach go crazy.

"Okay." Didi's lips pressed together into a thin line. "But if you want me to stay mad at Caleb, I totally will."

"Thank you. But you don't have to." Natasha hugged Didi. "Come on, let's focus. I love what you've done to the gallery!"

"Yeah? I still can't believe I'm showing at the Cove."

Instead of hanging the paintings traditionally on the walls, Didi had the canvases suspended from the ceiling, creating a rainfall effect but with art. There were thirty in all. From the looks of amazement on the faces of the people pouring in, Didi was making waves. And props to her brother for actually pulling off the servers dressing like the subjects of the paintings. Another home run for Nathan.

"Believe it." Natasha hooked her arm around her friend's shoulders in a show of solidarity. "I couldn't be more proud of you. No one deserves to be here more than you!"

Didi's blush was beautiful. She wore a black embroidered taffeta dress Nathan and Natasha had helped picked out, and she was styled to perfection, looking quirky but put together.

"I predict all the paintings will sell tonight," Natasha added.

Didi covered her cheeks with both hands. "Let's not get too excited. I might pass out."

"I just saw three of the top collectors in DoCo place stickers on your canvases. I'd say that's a great start."

"Excuse me," said a gentle, feminine voice.

With her arm still on Didi's shoulders, Natasha had to turn

both of them around to face Mrs. Winchester in a silver sheath dress. She had her hair in a neat bun at the back of her neck. Gone was the tired woman Natasha had spoken to in the kitchen, although in the deepest corners of her gray eyes still lay the sadness of a widow. Holding her hand was Albert, looking sharp in a navy sweater and slacks. He still looked confident despite his flushed cheeks.

"Mrs. Winchester," Natasha said in surprise. She unhooked her arm from Didi's shoulder and exchanged air kisses with the woman. "It's so good of you to come."

"When Albert told me about the success of his Entrepreneurship Day project, I just had to thank you in person." She took Natasha's hand and squeezed it. "You came at a time we needed you most. So thank you."

Heat blossomed in Natasha's cheeks. "Please, think nothing of it. Albert did most of the work. I was happy to help."

"She's being modest, Mom," Albert said, looking up at his mother with the adoration of a child.

"Oh, where are my manners?" Natasha said immediately, and gestured to Didi. "Let me introduce you to Diana Alexander. She is the artist of tonight's show."

"It's a pleasure to meet you, Diana," Mrs. Winchester said, shaking Didi's hand.

"Please, call me Didi. And thank you for coming." She smiled. "Natasha tells me you have quite the collection."

At first Natasha was nervous, since she wasn't sure how Mrs. Winchester would react. But the woman smiled and invited Didi to come over to their home to view their pieces. Didi immediately leapt at the opportunity, and they set a date.

"I was actually thinking of purchasing your portrait, Natasha," Mrs. Winchester said. "It's such a beautiful piece. But I'm disappointed to see that it's already been sold."

"What?" Natasha and Didi said in unison.

Mrs. Winchester nodded. "Yes. Which is why I had to settle for this one." She waved to Preston's portrait and placed a sold sticker on the plaque beside the canvas. "It's so provocative."

"Thank you, Mrs. Winchester," Didi said, complete awe in her expression.

It seemed she still couldn't believe that people were actually willing to pay for her art. Natasha hoped her friend would soon realize it wasn't a dream. That she was an artist worth her salt.

While Didi and Mrs. Winchester talked and Albert went to get drinks for all of them like a little gentleman, Natasha let her gaze wander from painting to painting. All her friends were represented. Nathan held a baton and conducted an orchestra confidently. Caleb sat on a throne made from yellow roses with his leg up on one armrest, his crown askew on his head. Each painting showed each individual in a different light yet captured who they were exquisitely. All of them were vibrant, so full of life. Natasha couldn't help but feel sentimental.

It had been an honor to pose for Didi. But at the same time, she felt uneasy knowing her portrait would be hanging in someone else's home. She wasn't completely sure she was okay with that. But she quickly pushed the unease away and held on to the feelings of happiness for her friend.

Her gaze landed on the entrance to the gallery just as Jackson stepped through the open doors in his version of edgy formal: a tuxedo jacket with leather lapels over a crisp white shirt and thin tie, slim pants, and wing-tip shoes. Her heart skipped a beat as he scanned the crowd, obviously searching for someone.

Her first instinct was to turn around and leave before he could find her. She breathed through the rising panic until she was calm enough to suppress the urge to run. She was staying. This was Didi's big night, and nothing could keep her away. Not even Jackson.

Eighteen

JACKSON'S HEART WAS pounding so hard that he thought he was going to be sick as soon as he stepped into the gallery Wednesday night. He had a clear plan of attack in his head, but a part of him wanted to chicken out. Nothing scared him the way Nathan did. And to ask him for his help? That was the height of insanity right there.

But, like Preston had said, Jackson needed to grow a spine and get shit done. This was for Natasha. This was for their future together. Surely Nathan would understand that. It was what got him Preston. He took a leap of faith. Now it was Jackson's turn to take the same risk.

He scanned the crowd. There were so many people.

Squaring his shoulders, Jackson waded through the masses, keeping an eye out for Natasha's twin. When he reached the center of the room with white walls and a black-tiled floor, a particular portrait made him pause. He turned to face it and it took his breath away. He could literally feel the air in his lungs being stolen, like a thief had come in the night.

It was Natasha in a dress that seemed to sparkle even if Jackson knew he was looking at a painting. She was standing in a crowded street, the only one different from the rest. That was exactly how he felt about her. She was one of a kind. And the painting captured perfectly the feelings of awe and wonder he felt for her every damn day. He could look at her all night.

Almost immediately, a sense of calm came over Jackson. He knew what he was fighting for. And as he'd promised, he would do anything—anything—to have her back in his life.

With renewed determination, Jackson forced himself to look away from the painting and search for the guy who held his fate in his hands. As if the universe was on his side, the crowd parted to reveal Nathan speaking to a server holding an empty tray in a corner of the gallery space. Jackson gathered all the courage he possessed and took a step toward him.

"You've got some nerve showing your face here tonight," Nathan said. His eyes were so cold his glare almost froze Jackson in place.

"Can we talk?" Jackson asked, glancing at the server. "In private."

The server walked away, not saying another word.

"I'm not giving you that satisfaction. If you want to talk, I don't see why we can't do it here." Nathan crossed his arms and didn't budge. "Look, I'm grateful for what you did in Rome last year. Those Maroon 5 tickets were a kind gesture. But that doesn't erase the hell you put Natasha through after you left and the hell you keep putting her through now."

"I know that," Jackson answered honestly. "You have to understand that I'm coming from a good place. I don't mean to hurt her. And I have no intention of hurting her ever again."

Nathan snorted. "You say that, but you're not the one who has to put her back together when she's sobbing on the floor because of some misguided attempt to win her back. Skydiving? Really?"

"You know she's always wanted to—"

"Of course." He cut Jackson off faster than a chef's knife cut through meat. "But that doesn't mean you should indulge her in that way. Look what happened afterward: she comes home to me in tears."

Jackson gritted his teeth. Nathan was angling for a fight. Over and over he reminded himself not to engage. Not to allow the fuse to be lit. He needed Nathan if he was to work things out with Natasha.

"Look," Jackson said. "I don't want to fight with you, Nate. I actually came here to ask for your help."

"My help?" Nathan touched the center of his chest and laughed. "That's the funniest joke I've ever heard. Not in a million years."

"I'm serious." He put all his intentions into his next words. "I know I hurt you. You were one of my best friends. You didn't deserve what I did."

"Of course I didn't deserve to be treated like trash," he said, hurt clear in his tone. "But this is not about me. This is about Natasha."

"I know." Jackson reached into his jacket pocket and pulled out a folded piece of paper. "Take a look."

Nathan glared at Jackson, then at the sheet in his hand. "What's that?"

"I want to prove to your sister, and to everyone, that I can be trusted. That I'm here to stay."

"Fine." Nathan snatched the paper and unfolded it. Then he gave it a quick glance. "What am I looking at?"

"It's a copy of the deed to the old music store," he said.

Nathan's lips pressed into a tight line. "What are you doing with it?"

"I just bought it."

For a long moment, Nathan was silent, studying Jackson like he wasn't sure he'd heard the words right. It was as if he was considering things carefully. A ray of hope shone through the dark clouds hovering above them for Jackson.

"I'm going to convert it into a studio," he continued, taking the opportunity to explain himself. "When I say I'm here to stay, I mean it."

"You bought the music store?" Nathan still sounded like he didn't believe Jackson, but his tone had lost some of its initial frostiness.

He nodded. "I want her back, Nate. I screwed up. I admit that."

"Then why are you talking to me about it?" Nathan handed back the piece of paper.

Jackson folded it carefully, choosing his words. "No matter what I do, it just looks like I'm hurting her even more. I need your help. Please, Nate, you're the one who knows her best. What can I do to get her to forgive me?"

There was another moment of silence until Nathan leaned his head back, both eyebrows raised. "Have you tried apologizing to her?"

The idea left Jackson shocked. How could he be such a fool? Planning the grandest gestures in the world and he hadn't thought to do the simplest, most important thing: actually tell her how sorry he was.

Jackson ran a hand down his face. "I'm such an asshole," he said against his fingers. "Why didn't I think of that?"

Nathan crossed his arms again and lifted his chin, a smug expression on his face. "Maybe because you're as dumb as a sack of rocks?"

The question brought with it feelings of inadequacy. What if he really didn't deserve Natasha because he'd forgotten the simplest thing? Then his gaze landed on the piece of folded paper in his hand. No. He still had to try. It needed to be something personal, something sincere. And he still needed Nathan's help to get it done.

While his brain worked, a prickle ran down the back of his neck. He knew what the feeling meant. As soon as he turned his head in the direction the feeling was coming from, he locked eyes with Natasha. She was standing across the room, staring right back at him.

Nineteen

THERE COMES A time in a man's life when he needs to get his shit together—even when faced with the unyielding gaze of the woman he loves. Maintaining eye contact, Jackson put one foot in front of the other slowly. Casually. In a nonthreatening way so he wouldn't spook her.

Natasha stood her ground. She looked amazing in a dark blue dress that brought out the bright color of her eyes. She wore the red lipstick he loved. And the shoes. Hot damn, they were sexy. The heels were high enough that they brought her at eye level with him, so if he did kiss her—not that he would at that very moment, since they both knew the consequences of their lips meeting—he wouldn't have to bend down to reach her lips.

He stopped about a yard away, giving her the space she needed to breathe without them being too far that she couldn't hear what he was about to say. Because what was about to come out of his mouth were the most important words in the world.

"What are you doing here, Jackson?" she asked tentatively.

"Tash, I've made many mistakes," he began, keeping his eyes on her beautiful face—the face he wanted to wake up to for the rest of his life.

"Where is this going?" A knot formed on her smooth brow.

"I was so focused on winning you back, I completely forgot the most important thing," he continued. He wanted to hold her hands, but considering how she was shifting her weight from one foot to the other, it might not be the best move, so he kept his hands to himself. "I'm sorry, Tash."

"What?" Her lips parted in shock.

"I'm sorry for breaking your heart," he said, putting all his sincerity into those simple words. Why had it taken him that long to realize? If he could kick himself, he would.

"Jackson . . ."

"You don't have to say anything. I just wanted you to know that I'm sorry. For all of it. And this time I want to prove to you how I feel." His mind worked on overdrive, coming up with the plan on the fly. "Meet me at the open field by the lake Friday night. Nine o'clock."

He began backing away, leaving her speechless. That was a good thing. He was afraid that if he said anything more, she'd bolt again. Let her think about it. The most important thing was that he'd put the plan in motion.

Nathan remained where Jackson had left him. Thank God, because he had no time to play Search for the Party Planner.

"How did it go?" Nathan asked, looking over Jackson's shoulder. "From the looks of things, she's frozen in place."

"Yeah, about that . . ." Jackson pressed his hands together as if in prayer. "I'm going to need your help."

"What did you do this time?"

"It's nothing like that. I just need the services of the best party planner in the world."

"Not quite." Nathan raised a finger. "But getting there. What do you need from me?"

Speaking fast, Jackson laid out his plans.

Natasha had no idea what had just happened. It was like a flash of lightning that left her temporarily stunned and blinded. Jackson had just apologized to her. Simple. Straight to the point. Then he'd told her to meet him someplace and walked away.

Just as she was coming out of her shook, she noticed the strangest thing of all: Nathan leaving the gallery with Jackson. How the heck did that happen? Not a day ago her twin was all but ready to bury Jackson in the woods somewhere. And now they were friends?

Natasha was so dizzy from trying to figure out each piece of the puzzle that Jackson laid out for her that she excused herself from the art show—but not before congratulating Didi once again. She figured her presence wouldn't be missed. Didi was entertaining all of DoCo, with Caleb proudly by her side. Natasha was happy for the both of them, but she also couldn't deny the fact that she envied what they had.

More confused than ever, she got into her car and drove home. In her daze, it seemed like she blinked and she was already home. She definitely wasn't thinking straight anymore. Maybe she just needed some sleep. So she went to her room and got ready for bed.

But after her shower, Natasha found herself sitting in front of her laptop, with YouTube showing all the searches for Jackson's songs. She had always kept up with his music before he left. After Amsterdam, she'd cut him out of her life completely.

She clicked on a song he'd released before Amsterdam. It was called "Stolen." As she listened to the upbeat dance music, her mind traveled to the first time they had kissed. They were at the WELCOME TO DODGE COVE sign the summer before their sophomore year. She remembered Jackson being so nervous that he almost missed her lips. A heavy weight settled in her chest.

When the song was over, YouTube immediately moved on to the next on the list. It was a newer song. Expecting another upbeat single, Natasha was surprised to find that "Inner Demons" was slow and sad. That was so unlike Jackson. He had always been so confident with his songs. Even if they were made for people to move to, the beats still showcased his love not only for what he did but for Natasha.

"Inner Demons" was dark, filled with longing. It called to something within her, pulling her back to those nights when she'd cried herself to sleep only to dream that Jackson had never left. And when she woke up to the reality that he really was gone, she'd find herself spiraling back down. The song somehow captured all those emotions, emotions she'd thought were felt only by her, not by Jackson.

By the time YouTube transitioned to the third song, called "Love Lost," it became pretty obvious to Natasha that Jackson hadn't been lying when he said that after Amsterdam he couldn't make real music anymore. Each of his new songs were like cries for help. Like he was searching for something missing in his life.

The corners of Natasha's eyes stung. Pretty soon tears were flowing down her face as she listened to song after song. Even when he was writing sad songs, it was clear that Jackson never once forgot about her. That even if he'd left to pursue his dream, she was always with him in the rhythm and beats he played every night for the horde of fans who enjoyed his work.

She was supposed to be happy, right? Happy that without her, he couldn't write a single worth a damn. She should be. Instead Natasha's heart was breaking for him. For the past six months, he had been miserable. Just like her. Even apart, they still were somehow in sync with each other.

Then the playlist switched to an older song. His first single with a music video, in fact. It had been viewed over a hundred million times. The fun beat was the perfect first-date song, which made sense, because he'd written it after his first date with Natasha: a drive-in movie by the lake. The stars were shining. Couples were snuggled together in their cars. The lake was calm and beautiful in the distance. It was the best first date.

As the song finished, Natasha clicked Pause. The video ended with Jackson looking straight at the camera. He was cradling his headphones between his shoulder and ear, and his hands were spread over the soundboard before him. The instant Natasha looked into those piercing golden eyes she knew: She was still in love with him. Unfortunately. Damn it.

Twenty

JACKSON WORKED THROUGH the night and all of the following day. Determination fueled him, along with the sandwiches and cups of coffee his mother sent up to his room. The song needed to be ready. Had to be.

By one in the afternoon on Friday, Jackson wasn't anywhere near satisfied, since he'd had to work with his old MIDI controller and outdated equipment. He missed being in a studio with a professional soundboard. Regardless, he needed to get some rest before the party he and Nathan were pulling together last minute. He rubbed both hands down his face. The song wasn't up to his usual standards, but it had to do. It was real enough. Honest enough. Made from who he was, where he came from, his history. The tweaks and alterations he had planned could wait.

Pushing back from his desk, he stretched, then stood. He had to be at the venue early to check on the sound system in place and brief the crowd on what he wanted before the party started. After setting his alarm for seven p.m., he stumbled to his bed, asleep even before his head hit the pillow.

Six hours of sleep, a bracing shower, and a hot dinner were all Jackson needed. He packed his things, got on his bike, and rode toward the grassy field on the other side of DoCo's man-made lake. He arrived at a little past seven. Why he hadn't thought to use the spot for a venue before baffled him. It was perfect. A little bigger than a football field, surrounded by pine trees. The lake's shore on one end. A parking lot several yards away. And the stage already built at the other. Barriers lined the area to ensure only one entrance and exit point.

Slinging his backpack over his shoulder, he headed for the simple platform. It wasn't what he was used to after a world-wide tour, but for his purpose it was perfect.

The sun was down. The stars were out. A great velvet sky blanketed them all. A long line stood outside the barrier into the field. The tweet he'd sent out the night of the art show worked. Mentioning that the party was free didn't hurt either. Jackson sighed in relief. So far, he had one thing going for him. As it was, he was nervous that Natasha wouldn't show.

Jackson tapped the closest security guard on the shoulder and asked, "Where's Nathan?"

The bulky guy went on the walkie attached to his shoulder and mumbled something. In two minutes Nathan came running toward where Jackson and the security guy stood. In slacks and a tangerine sweater, Natasha's twin stood out like a nail-polished sore thumb on that field.

"Oh, good, you're here," Nathan said, stopping and catching his breath. "The sound system you wanted just arrived."

"Good." Jackson breathed another relieved breath. Then his chest tightened. "Do you think Natasha will show?"

Nathan's eyebrow rose. "Are you nervous?"

"Fuck yeah, I'm nervous."

"Let's just focus on completing the setup. One thing at a time, or this party won't happen."

Jackson nodded. "At least let the crowd in."

"But we're not ready yet."

"Let me take care of what happens onstage. Anyway, I have to have a heart-to-heart with the audience. Might as well get them all primed."

Without hesitation, Nathan nodded at the security guy, who spoke into his walkie again.

"Your call," Nathan said. "Let's get you onstage."

Taking a deep breath, Jackson trailed after the bright sweater. The hand inside his pocket shook as he walked. Never in his DJ career had he been so unsure. It was like his first kiss all over again.

As he climbed up the metal steps to the stage after Nathan, they were met by a guy in a backward baseball cap and a T-shirt with a smiley face flipping everyone off.

"Arty," Jackson said, taking the man's hand and pulling him in for a back-patting hug. "Thank you for bringing the board on such short notice."

"Anything for you," he said.

"That's my cue." Nathan backed away. "I have a million other things to supervise."

As the crowd filled the field, Jackson shifted all his focus to the rig Arty had set up. All the goods were there. An MCX8000 with a solid metal chassis, dual hi-res screens, sixteen backlit velocity-sensitive RGB performance pads . . . basically, everything he needed and more.

Jackson hooked up his laptop to the beast of a controller. His fingertips were already aching to start playing. He shrugged out of his leather jacket and dropped it to the floor.

"You also have your speakers." Arty pointed at the large black Pioneers flanking them. "Everything is hooked up to the lights. No fog machine, sorry."

"That's fine," Jackson said, his focus already on making adjustments. He didn't even hear what Arty said before he left the stage. Everything needed to be perfect. For him. For Tash.

After plugging in his headphones, Jackson picked up the mic and faced the already full field. He brought the mic to his lips and said, "Hey, DoCo, are you ready to party?"

Hands in the air, the crowd cheered.

"To those of you who don't know me, I'm DJ Ax." He paused as another cheer filled the air. "And I'm going to need your help."

In a quick explanation, Jackson laid his heart on the line. A hush came over the partygoers. Hopefully, the payoff would be spectacular. The kind that sparkled in the night like a billion stars.

Once he was done, he said, "Let's dance."

Twenty-One

NATASHA SPENT THE two days after Didi's gallery show with Jackson's songs playing on a loop and doubting herself. One minute she wanted to run to him and say she had forgiven him, but the next minute all her doubts crept back in. What happened if she opened her heart up to loving him again and he left? She wasn't sure she'd survive a repeat of that night he'd stood her up at the ball for a chance at success in LA. Yet she knew everything he'd done—from coming home, to stopping time, to skydiving—was all to win her back.

He had said that whatever she did wasn't going to scare him away. That he was in Dodge Cove to stay. But things could change. What if he got a better offer? He honestly couldn't stay away from the music industry just for her. And she wouldn't do that to him. She might not know yet what she wanted to do in life, but forcing him to abandon his music just to stay with her was out of the question—she knew he would end up resenting her in the future, and then he'd leave all over again.

It always came back to him leaving. Her doubts. Her hesitations. It seemed like the end goal was the same: Jackson not in her life.

Around and around in circles she went until it was Friday night and the clock was ticking toward the time Jackson had told her to meet him. What could be at the open field by the lake? There was nothing there but grass and pine trees. Oh, and a parking lot. Yet she found herself dressing up anyway, choosing a maxidress and flats and braiding her hair.

Once she finished putting the final touches on her makeup, another wave of self-doubt sent her sprawling on her bed, staring up at the ceiling. Should she stay? Or should she go? What was the harm in going? But she knew if she did go, it was tantamount to admitting she had forgiven him and showing him that she still had feelings for him.

Her mind said one thing. Her heart said another. If only she could get them to agree.

The door to her room opened, but she didn't look to see who came in. Then one side of her bed dipped. That was when she finally faced her visitor. Nathan looked smart in a tangerine sweater, with his hair combed back.

"You're all dressed up," he said, a soft smile on his face.

She sighed. "I don't know, Nate."

"Is that one of Jackson's songs playing?" He glanced around her room.

Natasha turned it off. Instantly, silence flooded every

corner of the space. It felt weird not hearing the music after two whole days of listening to nothing else.

"Why did you leave the art show with Jackson?" Natasha asked. "You've been MIA since."

Nathan entwined his fingers over his stomach. "I thought I'd help out."

The admission caused Natasha to sit up and narrow her eyes at her brother. "You? Help out Jackson? What happened to being on my side?"

"Tash." Nathan stared straight at her. "I am on your side. That's why I'm here."

"What does that mean?"

"Do you remember when you were on the phone with me while I was in Ireland with Preston?"

She flopped back onto the bed. "How can I forget? It was a low point."

"Do you remember what you told me?"

"That love is like acid," she recalled. "It eats you from the inside out."

"Do you really believe that?"

Her eyes following the crown molding along the ceiling, Natasha thought about it. At the time, while she was heartbroken, it seemed true. Love did hurt. But she always knew that love could be magical too. It was the sunrise in the eyes of the one you loved. It was meeting your soul mate at six years old even if you didn't have words for the connection yet.

"Not anymore," she whispered, afraid that if she kept talking, the words would catapult her out of the bed.

"Then what are you still doing here?"

Immediately, she knew what Nathan was referring to. Because if her brother said he had lent a hand, then Jackson was definitely up to something. But the hint of curiosity wasn't enough. She needed more.

"I'm afraid, Nate."

There. The truth. In living color.

"We're all afraid." Nathan shifted to his side and rested on his elbow so he could look down on Natasha. "Didn't you think I was afraid when Preston whisked me away during the Society of Dodge Cove Matrons luncheon?"

"You?" She raised an eyebrow. "You're afraid of nothing."

"I wish." His lips quirked. "I'm just really good at rising above the fear. You need to rise above it too. If not for Jackson and what the two of you shared, then for the possibility of a future with him."

"Do we really have a future together? What if he leaves again?"

"He bought the old music store."

Natasha sat up so fast that Nathan barely had time to move out of the way to keep their foreheads from smashing into each other.

"What?" she asked, her voice between surprise and shock.

Nathan nodded. "He has plans of turning it into a studio. I saw the copy of the deed at the art show. I know that you're scared he's going to leave, but I think he's here for good. He's willing to put down roots—"

"For me," she interrupted.

"And what he has planned tonight." Nathan's eyes sparkled with barely leashed glee before he stifled a yawn with the back of his hand. "You should go, Tash. Everyone deserves a second chance."

It was like being given permission. For the first time since Jackson returned to Dodge Cove, it seemed Natasha's heart and head agreed. She didn't know if she wanted to laugh or cry. *No second chances* was what she'd told Jackson in Amsterdam. But, like the idea of love being acid, Natasha didn't believe that anymore.

She glanced at the clock. Fifteen minutes before their designated meet time. It would take twenty to get to the field by the lake. She bolted out of bed and grabbed her bag. At the door, she paused.

"Are you coming?" she asked, only to realize that Nathan had fallen asleep on her bed.

Twenty-Two

THE CARS WERE stacked one in front of the other. Good luck to anyone who wanted to drive away before the person blocking the way came. What was going on? Why were there so many people?

"What the . . . ," Natasha said, standing on her tiptoes as if to see where the dance music was coming from. It reminded her of the night Jackson had brought her to the club outside of town to watch him perform.

The crowd roared.

The hypnotic beats called to Natasha. A familiar song. It was almost as if it came from a siren's lips. Electric goose bumps climbed up her arms. Placing her hands on top of one another over her heart, she closed her eyes and bowed her head. The pulsing beat echoed in her chest. A *bam-ba-da-bam* that looped around, coaxing her hips to move. This was his music. His primal call. *Bam-bam-bam, bam-ba-da-bam, bam-ba-da-bam.*

Smiling, Natasha made a run for it. Toward the music. Toward *him*.

The security guard at the entrance waved her in before saying something in his walkie. She didn't pause to listen. She just kept going until she reached the edge of the crowd. The ground shook from the force of so many people jumping all at once. She jumped too, but only to catch a glimpse of Jackson onstage.

She had to get higher somehow, over the heads of the crowd. She glanced around until her gaze landed on massive speakers. A couple of girls were already dancing on top of one of them. She ran toward them and cupped her hands around her mouth.

"Room for one more?" she asked, shouting above the music.

At first they didn't hear her, so she slapped the top of the speaker until one of them looked down. Natasha was about to ask them for a boost when they both knelt and pulled her up by her hands.

What was Jackson planning? When Natasha left the house, she thought they would be alone. She wanted to speak with him. But from where she stood, he seemed so far away. A sea of people moved between them. The sight took her breath away.

Jackson was in full command of the crowd. His hands moved across the table, his fingers swiftly turning knobs and dials. With each new tweak, the song seemed to morph into something else. Pretty soon she was moving with the beat. There were metallic sounds. Whistles. Heartbeats. Whispers. And the sound of sonic booms. She imagined the universe having a sound and it was Jackson's song. Unlike anything she had ever heard before.

"This new song is amazing," one of the girls said, just as breathless as Natasha felt.

Natasha whipped her head toward the girl. "New song?"

"Yeah," the other one said, smiling. "DJ Ax is back!"

Natasha dropped to her knees and climbed down the speaker. She had to speak to Jackson. Right that instant. She couldn't wait any longer.

The second her feet hit the ground, she set off at a run through the crowd. She pushed and elbowed her way through, mumbling apologies for stepped-on toes or people shoved aside harder than she intended.

The easy way was to go around. Maybe she should have asked security to escort her. But Natasha felt in her revived beating heart that she had to go straight through. It made no sense. Love did that.

She had reached the middle of the field when a hand grabbed her arm, turning her around abruptly. A yelp cannoned out of her as she looked up to see a shirtless guy with long dreadlocks.

"Hey, you're Natasha Parker," another guy in a sleeveless shirt pointed out. "We went to school together."

Natasha tried her best to recognize him, but the lights were too erratic. All she could see were shadows.

"Weren't you with Jackson back in the day?" Sleeveless guy wagged a finger at her.

"Yes," she confirmed. "That's why I need to get to the stage. Will you help me out?"

Sleeveless guy shared a look with Dreadlocks, and they both grinned. In one heave, they hoisted Natasha onto their shoulders. She squeaked in surprise.

"What are you doing?" she asked breathlessly. "Put me down!"

"Pass her forward," someone shouted from below her.

As if on cue, a multitude of hands supported her weight. Her heart was beating so hard she thought she was going to pass out. But there was something so exhilarating about being carried over a crowd. She tilted her head up and watched the night sky and the stars that twinkled above them.

"Tash?" Jackson said, using the microphone.

Natasha twisted slightly so she could look toward the stage. Then she reached out for him. "Jax!"

He removed his headphones and rounded the DJ booth until he reached the edge of the stage. Several security personnel ran toward the edge of the crowd. The people in front handled Natasha over to the burly men as if she was a feather. They grabbed her by the arms and shoulders and lifted her up onto the stage, straight into Jackson's waiting arms.

She sucked in a breath the second her body met his. The scent of him enveloped her completely, igniting a spark that quickly turned into flames rushing beneath her skin as soon as their eyes locked. The people roared, caught up in the moment as much as Natasha was. Jackson was dazzling. His arms around her were strong.

"You came," he whispered against her lips.

But instead of falling into the kiss, as much as she wanted to, Natasha leaned her head back and said, "Jax, there's something I want to tell you."

"You don't have to say anything," he said. "I want to prove to you that I'm sincere."

"Jax, you don't—"

"No," he said, cutting her off gently. "When I came home, all I wanted was to get you back. I wasn't thinking about what you needed from me most. An apology. One straight from the heart."

"Jax . . ."

"Tash, I'm sorry." He looked into her eyes. "Will you forgive me?"

"Kiss her! Kiss her! Kiss her!" the crowd chanted to the beat of the music, arms in the air.

Cupping his face with both hands, she nodded and said, "Yes."

It was like the sun rose in Jackson's expression as he cradled the back of her neck with his hand. His lips were on hers before she could blink. She wrapped her arms around his strong shoulders, and it was like coming home.

A cheer reverberated into the night, sending shivers all over Natasha. She held on as Jackson deepened the kiss, claiming her. And she let herself be claimed. She put her heart on the line. She wanted the moment to last forever.

The lyrics—sung by a smooth masculine voice—hit all Natasha's senses at once. *"I will bring down the stars, bring down the stars for you."*

"What's that?" Natasha asked, breaking the kiss.

Jackson grinned. "This is what I wanted to show you." He set her down and returned to the DJ booth. Then he picked up the mic and shouted, "Bring down the stars."

All the lights and sound cut off. Natasha stopped moving, grabbing her chest. Her heart felt like it was going to leap out of her rib cage. She gasped as one by one the flashlights of what seemed like a million phones turned on.

From where she stood, in the darkness, it looked like a reflection of the sky on a clear night. Her lips parted. Her lower lids flooded, blurring her vision.

As a single tear fell down her face, Jackson said into the mic again, "I will bring down the stars. For you. Every single day of our lives together."

A flood of light came from the stage and the music swelled once more, bringing with it an awakening of the crowd. As if all at once, people started moving again, screaming and shouting. Hoots of joy filled the air along with the pulsating rhythm.

Looking at the sea of movement, Natasha fell in love as if for the first time.

Whoa! What a rush, Jackson thought as he pulled Natasha closer against his side. The girl he would love for the rest of his life had finally forgiven him. The look on her face the instant she did would forever be etched into Jackson's mind. He was never going to do anything that would intentionally make her sad ever again. At least, he would try his hardest.

He kept her close as he slowed down the dance party, afraid that if he let her go, he would wake up to find out it was all a dream. And Natasha didn't seem to mind. She stayed close without getting in the way. She knew the drill, and he loved her even more for that.

Jackson ended the dance party with a slow song. A sweet one. Then he thanked the crowd and bid them good night.

Once the lights went out, leaving only the soft glow of the perimeter lighting they had set up to help the partygoers to their cars, Jackson turned Natasha around to face him and wrapped his arms around her waist. As natural as April rain, she circled his shoulders with her arms and they swayed to the final beats of the song.

Jackson leaned forward until their foreheads touched. "I didn't think you'd show," he whispered.

"I didn't think so either," she whispered back, her breath touching his lips.

"What changed your mind?"

"Nate." She let out a soft laugh. "If you were able to coax him to the dark side, I knew you were sincere."

"You know what they say about the dark side," he said.

"What?"

"That we've got cookies."

"Jax." She rolled her eyes. Then, with all seriousness, she said, "Thank you for bringing down the stars for me."

"Tash, I'd bring down the sun and the moon for you."

"I'm starting to realize that."

"I love you," he said, voice breaking. He was exhausted and exhilarated at the same time. It was a miracle he was still on his feet.

"I love you too," she said.

Unable to hold back any longer, Jackson eased her chin up and kissed her. Again. And again. And again until they were both breathless.

Twenty-Three

JACKSON HANDED NATASHA his spare helmet the next morning. She stared at it at first, wanting so much to suggest that they take her car wherever it was he wanted to go, but the smirk of challenge on his face was what did her in. She shoved the helmet on her head and swung a leg over the bike.

"Any excuse to have my arms around your waist," she said, her voice muffled.

"And those damn long legs too," was his reply before he lowered his visor and revved the engine.

In seconds they were speeding along the Mallory Manor driveway and into the open road. Natasha's body felt awkward at first. It had been a while since she'd been on his bike. As if to tease her, he popped a wheelie as they headed into town. She squealed, squeezing him tighter. The bike bounced when he lowered the front wheel onto the asphalt.

"Jerk," she shouted.

"You know you like it," he teased.

He was right. As they sped by, she tightened the grip of her thighs against his and slowly let go of his waist, spreading her arms wide. Then, like she had done countless times before, she raised her arms above her head and shouted for joy at the top of her lungs.

Fifteen minutes later, Jackson was parking the bike in front of a two-story brick building at the edge of downtown. The large windows were covered with brown paper. She removed her helmet and stared up at the building.

"Did you really buy this place?" she asked.

Jackson removed his helmet and rested it between the handlebars. Then he reached back and took her hand, helping her off the bike, before he flipped the kickstand and swung his leg over. He placed his hands on his hips and breathed.

"Yeah," he said, a hint of nervousness in his voice.

He took her hand and entwined their fingers. Using her shock, he pulled her with him toward the front door. Fishing out a key from his pocket, he unlocked the door and pushed it in.

Despite the covered windows, sunbeams managed to find a way in, giving the place a spring glow. Dust floated to the floor like snow.

"Wow." Natasha turned in a tight circle, taking in the entire space. The hardwood floors were still in good condition. There was lots of room. Big windows let in natural light. It smelled musty, but nothing a quick cleaning wouldn't fix.

"Welcome to Underground Studios." Jackson spread his

arms out. "I've always wanted a studio of my own. A place where I can produce my music independently."

"That's huge!" Then her eyes widened. She ran into his arms and peppered his face with kisses. He laughed, holding her tightly.

"You're not leaving."

"I told you." He lifted a finger and tapped the tip of her nose. "I'm here to stay. Nothing you do will change that. I realized I can make music anywhere. I will still tour and there will be a ton of gigs, but my life is in DoCo. With my family. With my friends. With you."

"I feel like I have to do something," she said, pouting. "Help out somehow."

"Are you sure?" Jackson's eyebrow arched.

"I'm sure."

"All right. But you have to do something first." Jackson held up his index finger.

Natasha backed out of his arms. She clasped her hands in front of her. The pit of her stomach felt bottomless with a million knots in it. Lifting her chin, she told herself that whatever it was, she was ready.

"You have to promise to love me forever and ever."

She rolled her eyes. "What are we? Twelve?"

But he was serious. "Promise me."

Taking a deep breath, Natasha raised her right hand like she was about to recite the Pledge of Allegiance and said, "I, Natasha Parker, promise to love you, Jackson Fitzgerald Mallory, forever and ever."

He smirked. "Well, only time will tell."

"So full of yourself," she muttered under her breath. But

when she smiled, he smiled too. "Come on, there has to be something I can do." Then the idea came to Natasha's mind. "Let me help you set up this place."

Jackson rubbed his chin. "But don't you have events to help organize and attend? I can manage here."

Natasha shook her head. "Jax, when you left, I feel like I lost a part of me." She raised a hand, stalling him from saying anything else. "Let me get this out. You wouldn't let me speak last night."

"Okay."

She took a deep breath before continuing. "I slowly realized that planning and attending events is just a part of my DoCo life, but it's not what I want to do for the rest of it."

"College, then?"

"Maybe. But for now, I want to take things a day at a time. And the first task is helping you get this studio up and running. Who knows what will happen after that?"

He closed his hand over hers and pulled her forward until his arms encircled her waist. She placed both her hands against his chest, leaning away so she could look him in the eyes.

"Good," she said. "For a second there I thought you didn't need me."

He kissed her forehead. "I need you, Tash. I will always need you. Between us, we will take over the world."

He *needed* her. The word brought welcome warmth all over her body. To be useful to him, that was what she wanted. It felt right.

He took her hand once again and led her up the stairs to the second floor of the building. Several doors lined the hallway they entered. Jackson opened the second door to the left and ushered her inside.

Natasha gasped.

On the far wall of the huge open space was her portrait.

"You were the one who bought it," she whispered.

"Not at first." Jackson scratched his eyebrow with his thumb. "I bought it from the guy who did. I couldn't stand someone else having it."

Her heart melted all over again.

"What will this room be?" she asked. The space was cleaner than the one downstairs.

"My apartment," he said. "Eventually, I hope it'll be our apartment."

She turned away from the painting to face him. "Really?"

"This . . ." He pointed at himself and then at her. "You and me. This is it for me. Forever."

She held his face between her palms and leaned in for a kiss. Then she whispered against his lips, "Forever."

Then she turned around and faced the painting again. The possibilities were endless. With Jackson by her side, forever was finally figured out. The rest was easy.

ACKNOWLEDGMENTS

NO SECOND CHANCES came during an emotional time in my life. Little did I know that my hormones were out of control because of an undiagnosed illness. To say that writing this book changed and ultimately saved my life is an understatement. I honestly think that 2016 will go down in the annals of history as the year of no chill. It totally kicked me in the ass until the very end.

This book would not have been written without the help of so many people. First and foremost, I'd like to thank my mother. She hates it when I don't tell her things. So this is my promise to you, Mom. Open book.

Special thanks will always go to my amazing editor, Holly. Thank you for your patience and continued enthusiasm. I wouldn't be the writer I am today without your wisdom. And thank you for letting me get away with naming a minor character after a Winchester.

Lauren, your input always puts me at ease. Thank you for helping me see into my characters' souls. I am forever grateful.

My undying gratitude also goes to Kat. I wouldn't have thought of "it" that way if you hadn't showed me. My nose was too close to the screen to see clearly.

I would also like to thank Jean Feiwel and everyone at Swoon Reads for giving me a chance to share the Dodge Cove trilogy with readers. I'm so happy that Didi, Caleb, Nathan, Preston, and now Natasha and Jackson's stories are out there for anyone to discover.

Lastly, I would like to thank the readers. Without you these books would not have become reality. Thank you for your unfailing support. Reading your tweets and messages always makes my day. Thank you for welcoming the DoCo gang into your lives.

FEELING BOOKISH?

Turn the page for some

Swoonworthy EXTRAS

Natasha's Guide to Getting Over a Breakup

In the book, we see Natasha at a place in her life where she's exploring who she is outside of being with Jackson. Everyone goes through breakups. They can be messy. They can be mutual. It's the getting-over-it part that can be tough. Here is a list of things that might help:

1. Allow yourself to cry. Bottling up all that emotion isn't healthy, and it will only come out at the most inappropriate moment. So, cry. You'll think more clearly afterward.

2. They say eating ice cream and binge-watching your favorite shows in bed is out? Well, it works. Grab a pint of your favorite flavor and put on some *Project Runway*.

3. Talk it out. This is where your friends are a must. Don't shut them out. Welcome their concern after you've had time by yourself to cry.

4. Change your look. Time for a new haircut! Add some color. Have fun with it.

5. Retail therapy helps too.

6. Take that new look and new outfit out for a spin. Find the nearest party, and dance the night away. Bring your friends along. Endorphins are good for you.

7. It's time to unfriend, my friend. Purge that person from all your social media.

8. Learn to be single again, and enjoy it. Do what you like to do.

Watch that movie you've always wanted to watch. Go to the museum. Whatever. Just enjoy yourself.

9. Don't shut out love. Just because it didn't work out with that person doesn't mean you'll never find someone again.

10. Lastly, the pain does fade. Believe in that.

Jackson's Guide to Grand Gestures

Jackson plans elaborate grand gestures to win Natasha back big-time. He uses stopping time, defying gravity, and bringing down the stars as starting-off points. Of course, in the book, his plans are over the top, but there are still ways to surprise your special someone that isn't a typical date idea. Remember, it's the thought that counts.

Stopping Time: Plan a Picnic

This is a simple and easy way to hang out with your special someone that shows your planning skills. Here's what you'll need:

1. Pick a private, secluded spot. Someplace where the two of you can be alone without distractions or interruptions.
2. Find the perfect picnic basket. You can always ask your friends and family if you can borrow one. If you can't find one or prefer not to buy one, a regular bag will do.
3. Fill the bag with a meal for two. Think of the favorite food of your loved one. Nothing with mayonnaise because it can spoil easily. Sandwiches from a local deli are great. Cubes of cheese. Don't forget the crackers. Oh, and grapes. Just to name a few. Personalize. That is the key. It shows that you're thinking of what he or she might like instead of what you might like.
4. Pick a day. Make sure the weather is nice. But a little rain isn't so bad either.

5. Send your invitation. Not a text, mind you. A proper invitation with the time and place. Think romantic. It also doesn't hurt if you deliver the invitation yourself.
6. Enjoy the day. Spread out the picnic blanket, serve the food, and share each other's company. Put away your phones, and just talk. You'll eventually see that it's like time has stopped.

Defying Gravity: Indoor Trampoline Park

If jumping out of a plane isn't your style, but you still want to defy gravity, search for the nearest trampoline park in your area. It's a great way to bond and is so much fun. I'm pretty sure it will have the both of you laughing in no time. There are so many activities to try.

You two can open jump or join an ultimate dodgeball game, or you can even swim in a sea of foam. It's all about out-of-the-box thinking. Having fun in a way that isn't the usual dinner-and-a-movie dates. In the book, it's about spending as much time as possible together, showing that person how you feel any chance you get.

Bringing Down the Stars: Meteor Shower or the Planetarium

Check your local newspaper or the Internet for any news about meteor showers happening in your area. You can even combine the picnic idea above with this one, but make sure to bring a small telescope too. Imagine the two of you lying on the ground on a blanket and some pillows and just staring up at the open sky at night. It's a wonderful experience to share with the one you love.

A Coffee Date

between author Kate Evangelista
and her editor, Holly West

All About YOU

Holly West (HW): Who is your current book boyfriend/girlfriend?
Kate Evangelista (KE): I'm swooning over Oz from *Nowhere But Here* by
Katie McGarry. I really have something for guys on motorcycles. So hot.

HW: What's your favorite childhood memory?
KE: It's a Halloween memory. My mother bought me a jack-in-the-
box costume. It was the bulkiest thing ever, but I had so much fun
trick-or-treating that day.

**HW: When you were a kid, what did you want to be when you
grew up?**
KE: A doctor. I really thought I was going to be too because I got into
an honors medical course where you're a doctor in just five years.
But then I realized every time I thought about the symptoms of a
disease I automatically thought I was sick. Not good.

HW: What was your first job, and what was your "worst" job?
KE: My first job was teaching junior and senior high school English.
It was the best and worst job. I loved the teaching aspect of it, but
the paperwork was killer.

**HW: Do you have a breakup/makeup story of your own you are
willing to share?**

KE: I have one, but it's so heartbreaking that sharing it here might bum you and the readers out way too much after a Happily Ever After.

On Being a Swoon Reads Author

HW: What is the oddest thing a fan has ever said/done?
KE: Readers keep wanting to give me cats. Like kittens and a whole host of cats. I wish I could adopt them all.

HW: This is your third Swoon Reads novel. Have you got the process down now, or is it different every time?
KE: It's different every time, depending on the characters and the scenarios in the book. But I'm also understanding the process better and learning how to get to the story faster.

HW: This was the last book in the Dodge Cove Trilogy . . . What are your feelings now that the series is over?
KE: Bittersweet. I love Didi and Nathan and everyone. I'm going to miss them terribly, but I also know that they will all be okay.

HW: What question do you get most from your fans, and what question do you *wish* people would ask you?
KE: "When is the next book coming out?" And what I wish they would ask me? Well, what my favorite movie of all time is. It's *American President*, by the way.

Living the Writing Life

HW: How does the revision process work for you?
KE: At first, I get over the nervousness that initially comes when I

see an edit letter. I read the letter several times and make notes. Only then do I dive into the process. I appreciate the direction because I don't have to doubt myself.

HW: How has your writing process evolved since publishing your first and second books?
KE: It's become more open and informed. I have more control over the words and the characters inside my head. Is this what growing up feels like?

HW: If you could change one thing about your writing habits, what would it be?
KE: Less doubt, definitely. I hate second-guessing myself. I'm working on building my confidence, and that starts with being more open about who I am to myself and accepting that, yes, I am a writer.

HW: What writing advice do you have to share with the world?
KE: Finish. There is nothing to edit and publish if the novel isn't complete. Don't strive for perfection in the first draft. Just get it done.

No Second Chances

Discussion Questions

1. In *No Second Chances*, we find Natasha struggling to find who she is and what she wants out of life. What do you think she should have done differently after Jackson left?

2. The book revolves around the concept of second chances. If the person who broke your heart came back the way Jackson did and asked for a second chance, what would you do?

3. How would you describe Jackson's character in the book? Why do you think he left without saying a word?

4. What did you think of the grand gestures Jackson planned to gain Natasha's forgiveness? What would you have done if you were in Natasha's place?

5. What if Jackson realized all he needed was to apologize? What would have happened if he did earlier in the book? Put yourself in Natasha's shoes.

6. Jackson thought outside the box. What's a grand gesture that you would really appreciate and why?

7. If your friend was going through a breakup, how would you help him or her get over it? What is your go-to breakup remedy?

8. What do you think of Natasha still not figuring out what she wants out of life by the end of the book? What should she have done instead?

9. What would have happened if Natasha had moved on and was with somebody else when Jackson returned? Should he have given up on trying to win her back? Why or why not?

10. Where do you see Jackson and Natasha six months after the ending? Are they still together? What does their future look like?

One little lie turns into
so much more.

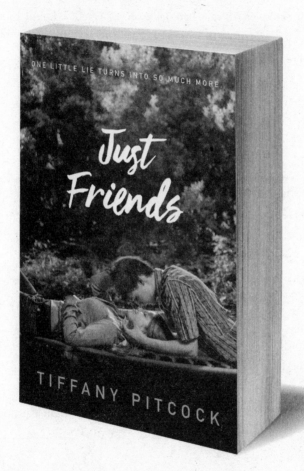

Chance and Jenny's friendship is based
on a series of elaborate lies, so how can
he convince her that his love is real?

*C*hance's Charger was still parked by the library, where he'd left it that morning. The black paint shone in the afternoon sun. Unfortunately, so did all the dirt clinging to it. *I should really get that washed.*

"I guess you've never been in my car before, huh?" Chance said as Jenny eyed it skeptically. He was wary of people judging his baby.

She circled it, scrutinizing it as she did so. "Of course I have," she said after she reached the passenger's side again. "I helped you pick it out."

Now it was her turn to make up a story. Chance unlocked the door, slipping into the driver's seat. "You did?" he asked after she climbed in.

"Mm-hm." She nodded. "You were unsure about it, you see, because it's so run-down with its ripped seats and messy floorboards. I was the one who convinced you it had character." She reached into her front pocket, producing a small tube of lip gloss. She flipped down the front visor so she could use the mirror. Chance watched as she applied the gloss—some cherry-red flavor, by the strong smell of it. She pursed her lips once before leaning up and pressing her lips to the mirror. She pulled back, revealing a single perfect kiss mark. "I marked my territory, see?"

Damn. Jenny definitely knew how to play the game.

Chance's eyes lingered on the kiss mark. "As my oldest friend, you always get shotgun."

She nodded, slipping the lip gloss back into her pocket. "Now everybody knows that."

He had to admit, the sight of her kissing that mirror made his heart hammer. He wasn't even sure *why*. For one, he had done a lot more than kiss other girls in that car. And yet none of them had gotten his heart going like Jenny and that mirror had.

Maybe it was because, in the back of his mind, he knew that this was the start of something bigger than those other things. That kiss mark wasn't a hasty hookup in the backseat of a car; it was precise—it was *planned*. It was, well, kinda permanent. Many people would pass in and out of that car, but that lip print would stay.

Jenny would stay.

NEED MORE DODGE COVE FUN FROM KATE EVANGELISTA?

SEE HOW CALEB AND DIDI FIRST MET IN

AND FALL IN LOVE WITH NATHAN AND PRESTON IN

Check out more books chosen for publication by readers like you.

When **KATE EVANGELISTA** was told she had a knack for writing stories, she did the next best thing: entered medical school. After realizing she wasn't going to be the next Doogie Howser, M.D., Kate wandered into the literature department and never looked back. Today, she is a graduate of De La Salle University–Manila with a bachelor of arts in literature. She taught high school English for three years and was an essay consultant for two. She now writes full-time and is based in the Philippines. kateevangelista.com